RUSH

A STONE KINGS MC ROMANCE

DAPHNE LOVELING

This book is a work of fiction.

Any similarity to persons living or dead is purely coincidental.

To my hero.

PROLOGUE

It all happened so fast, no one had time to react.

It was hotter than average that day, even for July, the thermometer topping out at ninety-four degrees by mid-afternoon. The townspeople had been going about their business, cars driving slowly down the main street of Lupine, Colorado, as if they, too, were turned sluggish by the heat.

There were muffled shouts coming out of the Blue Angus Bar, its door open to the heat of the day. Through the darkened threshold, Clayton Greenlee staggered into the blistering sun, already drunk despite the early hour. What came out of his mouth was mostly unintelligible, but the folks of Lupine were mostly used to that from Clayton, especially when it was clear he'd been on a bender.

But when Lester Lawson, a.k.a. Lawless, followed him out of the Blue Angus into the sunlight, the atmosphere soon began to change. A slight crackle seemed to give the air a sudden charge as Clayton's and Lawless's voices grew louder. A few people turned to glance at the men as they walked by, but most averted their eyes and walked just a little more quickly. As the men argued, Clayton's ramblings became more strident, and a word here and there began to emerge: "…whore…good for nothing….kill…" Most folks were still trying to pay no attention, but a few slowed down now, and turned their heads toward the men.

Suddenly, a sharp cry came from Clayton. He staggered forward and lunged without warning at Lucky. The wild swing of the drunken man's fist miraculously connected with Lawless's right temple, though not hard enough to take the large man down.

Those who had slowed to take a look now stopped: Lawless was not a man to be screwed with. He was the sergeant-at-arms of the Stone Kings, MC, the one-percenter motorcycle club based out of Lupine, and as such he was held in fear by all, and grudging respect by most. But Clayton was too either too drunk or too out of his mind to care.

Lawless's hand raised to Clayton's chest, and he pushed the other man backwards with a low growl. He muttered a few low, angry words to the drunkard, which only served to enrage Clayton further. "I'll fuckin' kill you!" he shouted, and reached into the back waistband of his dirty jeans. But before anyone realized what had happened, Lawless had drawn his own piece and fired.

Clayton's thin frame blew backwards like the wind had caught him. His heel caught against the curb and he fell into the street, his head making a sickening thud and crack against the pavement. A dozen or so shocked townspeople halted in their steps, then slowly wandered toward his prone form like zombies. No one was even talking or shouting, it had happened so quickly. As they people drew near to stare down at the wounded man, Lawless simply turned, calmly tucked his gun into his waistband, and walked away.

Slowly, slowly, the crowd began to grow. An ambulance was called, then the police. No one remembered calling his family, but about ten minutes after Clayton fell, a young girl broke through the gathering crowd — a girl of nine, maybe ten years old. Slight of build, wild brown hair streaming behind her, she ran wordlessly toward the figure lying in the dirt. As she skidded to a stop, she flung herself to her knees beside him. Throwing her arms around his heaving chest, a high pitched sob tore from her lips: "Daddy!"

The man lifted one feeble arm to touch the sobbing girl's head. Weakly, he began to cough, and in a wheezing whisper said something to the girl that no one else could hear.

Some of the men and women turned their heads away, then, at the shame of such a young thing having to see her father like that. Mothers covered their children's eyes. Fathers resolved to go home and hug their wives. But one child stood unnoticed in the crowd, unaccompanied. A boy, tanned and blond, about fifteen years old, stood and stared at the scene in front of him. He had been there all along, had seen it all transpire: the crazy drunken man who had threatened his uncle; his uncle, who had shot the crazy drunken man. And now the girl, sobbing over the prone, bloody figure. As the girl looked wildly around her, her arms still flung around her father, her tear-filled eyes met those of the boy. Their gazes locked, held a moment, until she squeezed her eyes shut in agony, her body wracked by her weeping.

The ambulance arrived. The crowd stepped back. Clayton Greenlee was pronounced dead at the scene as his daughter, still sobbing and screaming, was led away. The boy watched her go, and felt the rush of guilt and shame of one who realizes that his kin has been the source of someone else's sorrow.

In the coming days, the story would emerge of what had happened. Maggie Greenlee had been cheating on her no-good husband with Lawless Lawson. Clayton had somehow found out, and gone after his wife's lover, the drink making him foolish and careless. As the days turned into weeks, the town thought less and less of the young girl who had watched her father die, and of her two brothers who were also now down to one parent. The scandal became the stuff of gossip on front porches after dinner, the characters reduced to curiosities. For wasn't Clayton just a pathetic drunk anyway? And wasn't

Maggie, after all, just a cheating wife — and not a very friendly one, at that? She had never really made an effort to get to know her neighbors when the Greenlees moved to Lupine, after all. And what did she expect, getting involved with a Stone Kings member like that? No, it was sad all right, but somehow — and people never went far enough to actually say it out loud — hadn't they kind of had it coming?

CHAPTER 1

Seton

Fifteen years later

Some days it felt like everything was conspiring against me.

I had just finished up my shift at the Cactus, a local bar near the college in our town, and I was looking forward to getting out of my work clothes and relaxing at home for the rest of the evening. Stretching my aching arms over my head, I turned down the hallway to the back office to collect my purse. Just as I opened the desk drawer where I had stuffed it, my phone buzzed in my back pocket. I took it out and read:

Sorry see cant pick u up 2nite after work

I stared in disbelief at my phone screen, then sighed in frustration. It figured. I didn't even know why I was surprised anymore when Cal left me in the lurch. It happened more often than not. I swore softly under my breath.

Y not?

I waited a few seconds, not even sure if he would bother replying. Then the phone buzzed in my hand again and I read:

Club business. cant get away

Shoving my phone back into my pocket, I stifled a groan of irritation. Unbelievable. Not only was my brother not going to be picking me up like he promised he would, but he had my car to boot. And even worse than that, he was using it for just about the last thing I would have let him borrow it for if I'd known what he needed it for.

But then of course, I hadn't known. Because he hadn't bothered to tell me. Typical.

I walked out of the back office muttering to myself, and closed the door behind me. Closing my eyes in frustration, I leaned back against the dark wood paneling in the back hall. I considered my options. It wasn't worth chewing Cal out via text over what a shit for brains he was being. I knew if I called him, he'd just let it go to voice mail. Frankly, there was really nothing I could do at the moment.

"This is the *last* time I let him borrow my car," I seethed to myself. Grumbling, I reached for my pocket and pulled out my phone again. I typed in the security code and texted him back:

Forget it. I'll get a ride home.

A couple of minutes later, I got this response:

U mad?

My eyes rolled so far back into my head I thought they might stick that way. Seriously, I wasn't sure why I was even surprised at any of this. I could feel my blood pressure rising the more I thought about what to say in response. I knew he would barely read anything I had to say anyway. I decided to just forget about responding and try to concentrate on what to do next.

A wealth of less than charitable thoughts were swimming around in my head as I stomped my way back down the hall toward the bar area. My friend and fellow bartender Andi was just wiping down the counter. She looked up as she saw me plop down on a stool toward the far end of the bar.

"You okay, See?" Andi asked, one perfectly penciled brow raised as she looked at me speculatively. A perceptive girl, my bestie Andi is.

"Don't want to talk about it," I grumbled.

"Asshat stand you up again?" She cocked her head, her shock of short platinum blond hair falling forward over one eye.

I had to laugh at the irony that I had so many unreliable men in my life that Andi had to choose from a list. "No," I said. "My brother. And what's more, he has my car."

Andi blew her bangs back with an exasperated breath and chuckled. "That Cal. He's really something." Andi had the dubious fortune of having to listen to any number of my rants about my brother.

"That is quite the understatement, An," I smiled wryly. "Maybe I should start numbering the asshats in my life. Cal is Asshat Number One right now."

"You gonna call Asshat Number Two and see if you can get a ride out of him?" she smirked, tilting her head to one side.

Asshat Number Two was my boyfriend, unfortunately. Well, Nate was more or less my boyfriend. At least, I'd been sleeping with him on and off for about six months. He was good looking in a kind of "hot douchebag" way: thick, wavy blond hair that any girl would have killed for. Pretty blue eyes with long lashes, a perfectly sculpted gym rat body. He was firmly convinced he was God's gift to women, and probably half of the college girls in our town would have agreed with him. Lord knows why I had put up with him as long as I had. The sex had been pretty good, though somewhat lacking in variety, and he had caught me during a long dry spell, which probably explained why I had bothered to give him the time of day in the first place. But beyond that, he was pretty much worthless, rivaling Cal for unreliability. *Maybe I should start giving out douchebag trophies*, I snarked to myself.

Honestly, I should have kicked Nate to the curb a long time ago. As with many good looking men who know it (or at least so I've heard), Nate tended to be selfish in bed. It was probably sheer luck and horniness that I managed to get off with him most of the time. After he finished, he would look at me vaguely, say, "Good for you, babe?" and then slide out of bed to play Warcraft or something. On top of that, he was kind of a mooch. We had met at the bar one night while I was working, and he had started flirting with me shamelessly almost from the get-go. Only later did it occur to me that he might have been hitting me in the hopes of free drinks.

One of the things that sucked about Nate was that he was just so damn... affable. He seemed genuinely clueless about what a douche canoe he could be. It was like he just assumed the world would be charmed by him, and that assumption led him to believe he owed nobody anything. But he also had no temper that I could see, so I couldn't even get the satisfaction of a good fight when he let me down. He would never argue with me, no matter what went down between us. And even when he had done something so spectacularly shitty and irresponsible that I would explode at him in frustration, he would just grin at me and say, "Sorry, babe, I didn't know you'd be mad!"

So far, I hadn't managed to break up with him because he seemed to sense when he was on serious thin ice. On those rare occasions where he had a moment's worth of self-awareness, he would suddenly decide to do something sweet like pack us a picnic lunch somewhere. Never mind that that picnic lunch would likely consist of sandwiches from a convenience store and box cookies plus a couple of warm sodas. After all, it was the thought that counted, right?

Ugh. I honestly didn't know why I bothered with him. *Well, you do know,* my inner Jiminy Cricket reminded me. *Fine,* I argued back silently. *You don't need to be such a know-it-all.*

It's not hard to see you need to break up with him, Jiminy snarked back.

It's true. I thought glumly. I do. This was just too pathetic.

As if reading my mind, Andi put her hands on her hips, "I suppose you could call your dumbshit boyfriend to help you out, but I'm guessing he's not available either?"

I sighed. I didn't want to get into any of this right now. Andi had never liked Nate, and though she wasn't an "I told you so" type, she definitely had the right to be one. She had predicted that Nate would be bad news from the moment she saw him. Alone among all of my friends (not that I had that many) she didn't seem to be at all affected by his good looks or his boyish grin. She seemed to regard him as she would an undisciplined puppy who chewed the furniture and soiled all the rugs. His charm offensives had no effect on her whatsoever.

"Yeah," I said wearily. I took out my phone and looked at Andi with resignation. "Since I'm not going anywhere just yet, I might as well have a drink. Can you pour me a vodka and soda?"

"Lame-ass skinny-girl drink," Andi snarked. "If you're gonna drink, drink something that at least tastes like something."

"Just gimme my drink," I laughed as she turned and headed over to the rails to mix me what I'd asked for. I turned and spent a minute watching the crowd, a Thursday-night mixture of college students and townies. Funny how when I was working, I really never stopped to look at the customers who weren't sitting at the bar. People looked like they were having a good time. Men and women flirted; couples cooed and smooched. Parties of girls and guys laughed and jostled each other. It looked fun.

I texted Nate:

I'm stranded - can you come pick me up from work?

I waited a couple of minutes. Andi came back with my vodka and soda. Finally, my phone lit up with Nate's answer:

Sorry no can do. In the middle of a game

Of course. Some stupid third-person shooter game or something. Nate and his friends were obsessed with them. Apparently, "stranded" didn't mean much when his virtual buddies needed him.

Andi said as she watched me read my text. "I'm off in an hour. You want to come back to my place and hang out for a while?" she offered.

I looked at her affectionately. Andi was great about stuff like this. She would go to the ends of the earth for a friend in need. "Nah, it's okay," I said. "Maybe my roommate can come get me."

Andi shrugged. "No problem." Probably sensing that I didn't want to talk about my Nate problems at the moment, she nodded and headed down to the other end of the bar to help a customer.

As I watched her walk away, I remembered belatedly that my roommate Carly wasn't home tonight. Carly was a hair and makeup artist, and she had some gig going on in Denver's Art District on Santa Fe. She had done the makeup for one of the artists whose gallery showing was opening tonight, and the artist had invited her to the show to thank her. Since her family lived just outside of Denver, she had elected to go there after the opening.

So, assuming I ever got home tonight, I would have the place to myself. It figured that for once I had some privacy, and wouldn't have anyone to take advantage of it with. Shit.

Well, I supposed I could wait until Andi got off work, after all. I knew she would drive me back to my place. I'd just have to hear a lecture about Nate as the price I'd pay for the ride, because I knew she wouldn't be able to avoid saying something. "I told you so" person or not, I knew that Andi was worried about me. I supposed I should be grateful someone was.

Were all men this unreliable and ridiculous? I wondered as I sat there sipping my drink. I hadn't had all that much experience — my entire sexual history tallied up to the astounding number of three whole men. But every one of them had been kind of... not *there*... in some way. One was my high school boyfriend, who blushed furiously when he asked me out for the first time, and with whom I lost my virginity silently in his parents' basement one afternoon. The second was my boyfriend during my sophomore year of college. We hooked up midway through spring term, and seemed to only see each other when he came to my dorm room for Saturday night booty calls. We broke up at the end of the school year, and since I had had to drop out of school for lack of tuition money, I hadn't seen him again. And now, Nate. Honestly, the worst part was, Nate was kind of the best of the bunch. *Is this what I have to look forward to?* I wondered. Just a long string of unfulfilling, boring half-relationships? Maybe I just needed to get myself a bunch of cats and call it a day.

Maybe there was just something about me that just attracted irresponsible men. Certainly, my own family life was no model of happy relationships. My older brother Reed... well, who knew where Reed was. He had been my idol when I was growing up, but now... He had left home at sixteen and had made himself scarce ever since. He would be twenty-eight now, and I hadn't seen him in at least five years. Rumor had it that he was living somewhere north of Denver, and even that he had done time on some sort of assault charge, but I had no address or phone number for him.

And now my younger brother, Cal, was looking like he wouldn't turn out much better.

I had never seen Cal care about anything, frankly. He had always been irresponsible, and had a streak of resistance to authority that ran deep as a river through him. He had spent almost more time in juvie than out of it as a teenager. He had graduated high school last year — just barely — in Scottsdale, where my mom lived now. After he graduated, he came back here to Lupine for some reason, and had seemed content to just party and work menial jobs. I hardly ever saw him except when he needed a favor. Cal couldn't be relied on for anything. He took nothing seriously, and ducked responsibility like it was a disease.

Until now, ironically. Until the Stone Kings Motorcycle Club.

Ever since he had gotten the leather vest with the patches that said "prospect" on the back ("It's called a cut, not a vest. And they're called *rockers*," I could hear Cal correcting me in my head), he had gone from being a wild, reckless kid with a defiant streak to a cocky, self-important ass. Nothing else seemed to matter to him but the Stone Kings MC. Every time I had talked to him in the last few months — not that that was very often — he would respond only evasively to any questions I asked him. His only focus was getting into the MC as a fully patched member, and he couldn't be bothered to give a damn about anything else. Certainly not anything as mundane as coming through for his only sister, the only family member who currently seemed to care about him or his whereabouts.

He was clearly on some sort of mission tonight for the motorcycle club he was trying to join. I couldn't see that going anywhere good. We hadn't had an actual conversation about what the hell kind of business he was doing for the Stone Kings. Every time I had tried to bring it up, he waved me off, saying the club was a brotherhood, and he had to prove himself so they knew they could rely on him. That the club wasn't what I thought it was.

How the hell did he know what I thought it was? I knew one thing about it. The only thing that mattered: it was a member of that very same MC that had killed my father.

I couldn't figure out why Cal didn't seem to care about that. But I never got the chance to ask him before he was off to do some job or other for them. Hell, he didn't even have his own motorcycle yet. Hence why he had my car tonight.

I grabbed my glass abruptly and took a long drink, savoring the feeling of cool, flavorless liquid and searing carbonation burning my throat. Enough thinking about all of this for one night, I told myself harshly. I wasn't going to solve my problems sitting here brooding. I stood up and took my empty glass with me as I walked back behind the bar. I grabbed the apron I had stowed on the shelf and put it around my waist.

"What are you doing?" Andi asked, glancing over at me from the cash register.

"I'll help you close the bar if you'll drive me home afterwards."

Her eyes widened. "Nice! You're on! It'll be sweet to be out of here a little earlier. I can use the extra sleep. Early practice tomorrow." Andi was a budding singer and songwriter, and performed at various venues around town with a local band called the Nopes.

A couple of hours later, Andi dropped me off at my apartment. I noticed wryly as I walked up the front walk that Nate hadn't bothered to drop off my car. "You sure you don't want to come home with me?" Andi called again from the open passenger window. "I know it's late, but just in case you don't want to be alone…"

"I'm fine, Andi. Really." I smiled reassuringly at her. "Don't worry. I'll see you Saturday." We often worked together on weekend shifts.

"Sounds good. Have a good one, chica!" As she rolled up the window of her dark blue Kia, I heard the sound of the radio being cranked up. She put the car in gear and drove off, head bobbing ferociously to Pink. I grinned in spite of myself and walked up the sidewalk to my building.

The apartment was dark when I got in, so I knew that Carly hadn't changed her mind and come back home after the gallery opening. She was an unapologetic night owl, so no way would she be asleep yet. I dumped my purse on the chair beside the door, flipped on the light and looked around. Despite the late hour and the long work day, I wasn't tired at all.

Aimlessly, I walked into the kitchen and opened the refrigerator. After digging around for a minute, I found a half-eaten pint of cookies and cream ice cream. It seemed like the sign that a comfort food and movie session was in order, so I sat down to watch one of my favorite old movies: *City Lights*, by Charlie Chaplin. I discovered it my freshman year at college, when the campus had scheduled a silent movie series, and I must have watched it over a dozen times since then.

I sat quietly watching the movie with its strangely affecting music, laughing at the funny parts. And crying like a baby at the end, when the little tramp's love interest finally realizes that he has given up everything to make her happy.

CHAPTER 2

Grey

It felt good to be home. Mostly.

"Grey!" my VP, Trigger, shouted as I walked through the door of the clubhouse bar. About half a dozen members of the Stone Kings MC turned toward me. "Fuck, brother, we didn't expect you back for three, four more days," Trigger continued.

"Yeah, well, I couldn't leave the club in the hands of you bunch of pussies, now could I?" I snarled. A chorus of raucous laughter greeted my words.

Trigger came up and gave me a big bear hug, clapping me on the back, and I returned the favor. A few other members of the Stone Kings gathered around me and called their hellos: Levi, Repo, Tiny... A few of the club whores were around, as well, and one or two nodded and winked their open invitations at me. The men and I exchanged a few minutes of pleasantries as I got caught up on news of this member's pregnant wife, that one's recently sick kid. Eventually, the crowd dissipated a bit, and I turned back toward Trig and pulled him aside.

"How you doin' brother?" he grinned as he stepped back to take a look at me. "The cabin treat you good?"

"Yeah. It was fine." I nodded at his beer. "Let me get one of those and let's you and me talk about what's gone on in my absence."

I walked over to the bartender of the moment, a peroxided blond named Tammy, and grabbed a bottle for myself and another one for Trig. "Here you go, Grey," she said, making sure to lean way over so I could see down her shirt. Those tits were fucking fantastic, I knew from personal experience. Of course, they should be, as much as she probably spent on them. I smiled. "Thanks, Tam." She winked back.

I turned and gave Trig a chin nod, motioning him over to a private table at the back of the bar.

"What's up?" he asked as he slid into a chair. He leaned back and took a long swig. "Like I said, we weren't expecting you back so soon."

"Yeah, well, I got bored," I retorted. Not exactly true, but it may as well stand in for the truth. I'd been gone for close to three weeks, and the truth was, sitting there alone with my thoughts up in the cabin had started getting the better of me. Eventually I figured it was better to get back here and face the music. My head was on straight enough, I guessed, in spite of what had happened. At least I hoped so. It had to be.

"So," I continued. "Any more news since we last talked?" Trigger had phoned me two days ago with a short update.

"Nope," he answered. "Nothing much has changed since you left." He laughed, a short, dry sound. "Hammer's still dead. And the boys took care of Jethro, just like you ordered."

I winced at the mention of Hammer, but nodded. "Good. All the evidence been disposed of?"

Trig grinned wryly. "You know it."

Jethro had been one of ours. At least, we had thought so. That son of a bitch betrayed each and every one of us. He was the one responsible for Hammer's death. That piece of shit fucking ran from the scene instead of staying to fight with a brother. He left Hammer to fucking die.

I had been the one to let Jethro into the club when he patched out of my uncle Lawless's club in Reno, and I had beaten myself up for it every goddamn day since Hammer was killed. Hell, I not only let him in, I had lobbied for it, and even convinced a couple of the other brothers when they weren't sure about him. Ultimately, I had betrayed the club's trust by pulling in someone I shouldn't have. I had let my judgment be clouded because he came recommended by a family member. I was fucking bound and determined to make up for that.

I swore to myself that I would not let my judgment be clouded ever again.

Going forward, I knew that what happened in the coming weeks and months was crucial. It was one thing to take Jethro out. That much was necessary, but it wasn't enough. As club president, it was absolutely fucking essential that my brothers knew I was not afraid to take out the most exacting vengeance for a traitor in our midst. To show them this would never happen again, and that no one — *no* one — was above the law of the Stone Kings. Before I let anyone else in this fucking club again, I would be goddamn sure of them. No matter what.

"So," I continued, "We any closer to finding out who killed Hammer?" Shit. Hammer. My best friend. More a brother to me than my own brother. Just thinking of it put a load of ice in my stomach. It had been a month, and I still couldn't believe he was gone.

"Still pretty sure it was the Cannibals. Nothing has happened since you left, though. We still got no real proof." Trig took a long pull of his beer. "But who else would it be?"

I thought about it. The Cannibals in theory were our biggest potential problem at the moment, since their territory butted up against ours. If they wanted to make a play for, it they could be the biggest threat to our arms territory. But things had been relatively calm on the Cannibals front for a while now. It didn't make sense that all of a sudden this would have boiled up to the surface. Unless something was going on that I didn't know about. Unless there had been some sort of plan in place for longer than I had realized, and it was just now starting to show itself.

When Hammer had been killed, my first instinct had been to end anyone and everyone who could have had something to do with it. Problem was, we had no idea who that was. That was part of the reason why I took off for a bit: to cool my head. I knew Trig could handle the club in my absence, and I knew he'd call me immediately if any shit started to go down. I could make it here from the cabin in less than an hour. I'd spent my weeks up there trying to get some distance, to think it all through. I still hadn't come up with anything. Which is why I'd come back. Now that my anger had cooled, it was time to pursue those responsible with a cool, clear head.

"Yeah, okay. I'm with you that I can't figure out who else but the Cannibals it could be. But I wanna be sure. Absolutely fuckin' sure."

"You and me both, prez. We've been doin' some recon while you were gone. Not much to report, but Levi and Repo can tell you what we got." He glanced over at the bar and nodded toward them.

I took a deep breath and let it out. "Okay. We're gonna need to have church tomorrow to talk more about what to do about this. As for tonight, though, I'm in the mood to have a little fun." That was bullshit. I was in no fucking mood to party. But I figured the guys needed to see me, there with them. They needed to see that I had straightened out my head and was ready to go. That the loss of my best friend hadn't made me weak. Being the president of an MC was about more than leading. It was about showing no fear in the face of danger.

"I hear you, brother," Trigger agreed. "We'll set up some shots in Hammer's honor, and get this party started."

"Do it," I nodded. "By the way, how the new prospects lookin'?"

Trig shrugged. "Dunno. They look like fuckin' puppies, they're so young. The one, the guy who looks like Frankenstein, I guess he's okay. He doesn't say much. But he doesn't bitch no matter what you ask him to do, either, so that's a plus."

"Frankenstein's monster," I said.

"What?"

"It ain't Frankenstein. It's Frankenstein's monster. Frankenstein was the scientist."

"Fuck you, Grey."

"Hey, I can't help it if you're an ignorant bag of shit. Go read a goddamn book."

Trig twisted open the second bottle of beer he'd brought with him and chucked the cap with me. "I got no time to read a book. I'm knee deep in pussy, brother."

I laughed. The first real laugh in a week. God, it *was* good to be home after all. "What about the other prospect?"

"Cal? He's okay. He's full of shit, but he's a funny dude. Got his eye on half the club whores already," Trig grinned.

"He better slow his ass down," I remarked with a frown. I finished my beer with a final swallow. "He's got more important things to do than chase tail."

"Brother, ain't no more important thing than chasin' tail," Trig corrected. "Besides, it ain't exactly 'chasin'', now is it? Most of these girls'll give it up for anyone in the club, no problem. 'Sides, Cal's not a bad-lookin' dude. Most of the time when he's lookin', they're lookin' right back."

"Good lookin' is he?" I cocked my head. "Maybe you want a go at him yourself?"

"Brother, you better watch yourself if you don't wanna get cracked over the skull with this bottle," Trig warned, but he was smirking as he said it. Trig could give as good as he got, but he could take a joke.

I looked out at the bar as more of the brothers wandered in. "Hey, Tammy!" Trig yelled. "Set up some shots for everybody. We're gonna drink to Hammer's memory!"

"Will do, Trig!" Tammy yelled back. A chorus of yells followed. Time to get the party started.

"Well, we'll see about these prospects," I said, looking at my VP as I stood up. "I'm gonna be ridin' the hell out of 'em. We can't afford to take any more chances. After what happened."

Trig looked me in the eye. "Agreed. "

"All right, enough talk. Let's party. I need to shake this road dust offa me."

"Yeah," Trig said with a shit-eating grin. "Let's go see how many shots the prospects can take before they puke their guts out."

CHAPTER 3

Seton

The next morning, I woke up on the couch with an empty ice cream container sitting on the coffee table. Next to it was my phone, and I checked it to find another text from Cal, saying my car was in the parking lot of a local bar owned by the MC. I actually laughed, it was so ridiculous. I supposed I should be grateful that he actually included directions on how to get there. The location of the freaking Stone Kings Motorcycle Club was not exactly on my radar, and I was pretty sure it wouldn't be on Google Maps, either.

I was feeling pretty sorry for myself, but it was Friday and I had most of the day off, so I decided I needed to take advantage and try to get some things done before my evening shift. Even though I didn't normally eat breakfast, I made myself a plate of eggs and hash browns to fortify myself. I even brewed half a pot of strong coffee, which I drank while sitting on the window seat in the living room and staring out at the street. It was early summer, and school had just gotten out, so of course there were little kids riding around on bikes and yelling crazily, letting off all the steam of the school year in one go. It was fun watching them. I kind of remembered being like that myself, but it was so long ago. Every carefree moment of my childhood seemed to have come screeching to a halt when my dad was killed the summer I was nine years old.

My father. Clayton Greenlee. The town drunk. Well, I suppose technically he probably wasn't old enough to be the town drunk. Don't town drunks have to be old? But that's where he was heading, anyway. He probably would have died of the drink eventually, except that something else killed him. Something else entirely.

At the time, I was too young to know that the town thought of him that way. I didn't even know what an alcoholic was. All I knew was that he and my mom fought about his drinking a lot. If Clayton and Maggie Greenlee had ever been happy together, those times were long gone by the time I had any memories. Mostly, I just remember the arguments, and of those arguments, I mostly remembered my mom's criticisms. I knew that she blamed him for having to go to work after Cal was born. I knew she was angry that he had trouble keeping a job for very long. I knew she considered him half the man she had thought he was when they had met.

But I didn't really know or care about any of those things. Because to me, he was my daddy, my hero. Any weaknesses he had, I looked right past them and saw only the way he smiled at me, ruffled my hair and called me his SeeSee.

Growing up the middle child between two brothers, I often felt out of place. Reed and Cal preferred playing with their own rambunctious classmates to spending time with their boring sister who preferred reading to sports. My mother seemed to choose her solitude over spending time with her only daughter or teaching her things. To be fair, it wasn't just me she ignored. Maggie Greenlee never seemed to really take to motherhood. When my brothers and I were young children, it seemed like we were always trying unsuccessfully to get her attention. Whenever she did seem to notice us, it was usually to yell at us for messing up the living room or spilling milk on the kitchen floor. But whereas my mom could be volatile, aloof and temperamental by turns, my dad was always constant, doting and affectionate with me. He loved me, and I always knew it. His affection was the center of my world.

Most of my memories of my father were hazy now that I was an adult: a hand on my head, the smell of his beery breath when I came home from school, his raucous laugh when he would tell me little-kid jokes. But by far my strongest, most vivid memory of him was when he died at my feet, in the street. Shot by my mom's

lover, a member of the local biker gang. The Stone
Kings.

In the weeks leading up to his death, my parents had
been quarreling more and more. I'll never know how
long my dad knew about the affair, but I remember him
coming home drunk more often, and that he had a
haggard look in his eyes that I had never seen before.
Then one day, just as school was letting out on the
second to the last day of the year, Reed came running up
to me as I was walking off the school grounds and told
me Dad had been shot.

I got to my father just moments before he died. I still
remember being shocked by how ashy gray his skin was,
and how vivid the crimson of his blood looked by
comparison. As he wheezed his final breaths and I clung
to him, he whispered something to me that I couldn't
catch through the sound of my own sobs. I opened my
mouth to ask him what he had said, but he was already
gone. It still haunts me that I didn't know what the last
words he ever said had been. I felt like I had failed him
by not hearing them.

As unknown hands were pulling me away from my
father's body that day, my eyes ran unseeing over the
crowd of mostly adults, until suddenly they locked on
the eyes of another child. I remember he was a boy, of
about Reed's age. A wave of anger hit me so intense it
almost knocked me back to the ground. It was a
blinding, rabid fury at him, whoever he was, for being a
child like me, but who probably still had a father. Who
would probably sit down to dinner that night with him,

and tell him about school, and his father would ask him whether he had any homework. Things I would never have again.

After the funeral four days later, my father's name became all but forbidden in our household. It wasn't that my mom ever said that, exactly, but somehow it was clear to all three of us kids. I didn't want to talk about him much, anyway. My pain was too deep, too private, to share with anyone. My older brother Reed became sullen and withdrawn. My younger brother Cal asked for my father a couple of times in the first days, but after being hushed angrily by my mother, he eventually stopped. I retreated to my room, and tried to pretend that my daddy was still there, that he was simply at work and would be coming home soon.

The story behind my father's death traveled quickly through the town's gossip circles, and we became the subject of feverish whispers. I was too young to understand exactly what had happened, why my father had been killed, but I knew that people were saying whatever had happened was because my daddy was Bad, and my mommy was Bad, too. The town whispered about it when I or my brothers would walk by, to the drug store to buy candy, or walking home through downtown after school. Our family had the whiff of scandal about it now, and everyone knew the name Greenlee, though few talked about any of it to our faces.

My mom grew even more remote after my father's death. She had never been a particularly affectionate mother, anyway — as an adult, it seemed a mystery to me why she had had kids in the first place, given that most of the time she just seemed irritated by the mess we made or the noise we caused. But whereas before that day she had yelled at us frequently, afterwards it was almost as though we didn't exist. Reed was just old enough to babysit us younger kids, and so Mom began to leave us fairly often to fend for ourselves in the evenings. We didn't know where she went, but it didn't seem to be in Lupine, because we probably would have heard about her goings on from other people in the town if they'd known anything. Reed would put us and himself to bed, and then in the morning, she would be back, and no one would talk about when she had come home or where she had been.

Eventually, my brother Reed left home at seventeen, moving in with the family of one of his friends until he could finish high school. My mother didn't protest. Once he turned eighteen, he left the area, and we had only had sporadic news from him after that. Barely three months after I graduated from Lupine Senior High, my mother packed up and moved to Scottsdale, Arizona, leaving me with a junker car full of possessions to drive myself to my freshman dorm at Aspen College. My younger brother Cal, who had just turned thirteen, went with her.

I spent my freshman year of college mostly alone, save for the occasional terse hand-written letter from Scottsdale with a couple of twenty-dollar bills inside. I went "home" for the summer, but it didn't take long for me to figure out my mom didn't really want me around.

Away from the taunting gaze of Lupine, she had found a new life for herself with a perpetually-tanned dentist named Darryl who smiled too much and laughed too loud. He put up with Mom's moods, though, I had to hand that to him. And really, he was nice. But I felt out of place, and Cal was just old enough to have found himself a crowd of teenage boys to hang out with, and he was rarely around. So, I went back to school that year, and when I ran out of money to live on spring semester, I didn't ask my mom for help. Instead, I took a leave of absence and decided to get a job to save up the rest of my tuition money myself. Somehow, I ended up back in Lupine, and three years later, here I still was, working at the bar and saving for a future I didn't even know if I wanted.

I finished up my coffee and my musings and went to take a shower. When I got out, Carly had come back. "Hey, girlfriend!" she called to me cheerily.

As always, Carly looked supremely fashionable, her curly riot of blond hair mussed just to perfection, her makeup stunning without being overly noticeable. She was wearing a tight black dress and dark knee-high Frye harness boots. The exquisitely-done Mayan-design sleeve tattoos on her arms somehow made her look only more elegant. In my formless bathrobe and wet, straggly hair, I felt like a schlub next to her. It was a good thing she was so nice, I told myself, because otherwise I would have felt like strangling her.

"Hey, you're back!" I replied. "You want some coffee?" I asked, nodding over to the maker. "There should still be a cup or so left."

"No thanks," Carly said, plopping down on the couch and heaving a long, dramatic sigh. "Man, I am *bushed*! What's up?"

"Not much." I decided to spare her the pity party of me whining about my last twelve hours or so. "I thought you weren't going to be back until Sunday."

Carly rolled her eyes and grinned at me. "Yeah, I know. But my mom was already driving me crazy." I had met Carly's mom a couple of times, and to me, she seemed perfectly nice, but I knew she and Carly clashed over her career choice. "Besides, I ended up getting a last-minute wedding gig tomorrow. A friend of mine who is doing the wedding needs a hand because her assistant backed out at the last minute. So I have to go do a practice run with the bride and bridesmaids today."

"Cool," I said. I knew weddings tended to pay well, even if they were very time-consuming and could be stressful.

"Yeah. The money's cool, anyway," Carly admitted. "I hear from Gabi that the bride is kind of a bridezilla. So I'm sure she'll be pissed that I'm coming in last-minute."

"You'll wow them," I assured her. And she would. I had seen Carly's work. She was amazing at what she did. And passionate about it. Watching her grow more and more in demand as a hair and makeup artist made me wish I had some idea what I wanted to do with my life.

I bent over and gave my hair a good towel-drying. "You shouldn't do that," Carly said mildly. "It's damaging to your hair. You're roughing up the cuticle."

"So you've told me," I grinned. I was used to Carly's beauty hints. If only I followed half of them, I was sure I would look ten times better than I did, but I was just not that much of a girly girl at heart. Laziness usually overtook most of my best beauty regime intentions.

"You should really get a micro-fiber towel. Those things are amazing." Carly kicked off her boots and put her feet up, leaning back against the sofa pillows. "So, what's your story? What do you have going on today?"

I told her I had to go pick up my car, and why, and she was appropriately sympathetic. She did offer to drive me to the bar to pick up my car, though, which was super nice of her, because otherwise I'd have to walk or figure out whether there was a bus that went by there. I ran to the bathroom and dried my hair, pulling it back into a loose pony, then went to my bedroom and changed into a white t-shirt and some shorts. I wasn't really in the mood to put on any makeup so I decided to skip it. By the time I was finished changing, Carly was ready to go, too. I gave her directions to the address Cal had given me as she drove. Turned out the clubhouse was about four miles away, in an area of town I hadn't spent a lot of time in.

"There's your car," she said, pointing. Sure enough, there it was. In a parking lot full of Harleys of different sizes and shapes, my aging Mazda stood out like a sore thumb.

I thanked Carly for the ride, wished her luck that afternoon, and got out. Walking over to my car, I suddenly realized two thing: first, I had forgotten my spare key. And second, I had no idea whether Cal would even think to leave the set he had in the car for me. I groaned in exasperation. If I had come all the way here only to not be able to pick up my car after all, I'd have a four mile walk to get back home.

I reached the car and tried the driver's side door, which opened, thankfully. But when I got in, I didn't see the keys anywhere. I looked under the floor mat, and above the visor. No luck. I checked the glove box, but they weren't there, either. Frustrated, I sat in my car with the door open for a couple of minutes and tried to think what to do next.

"You lost?" a deep voice said beside me, making me jump. I looked up, and locked eyes with one of the biggest men I'd ever seen.

He looked down at me with strangely intense dark eyes, his expression unreadable. His hair was close cropped, his jaw square and hard. A shadow of a beard just made his features more striking. He was wearing a black t-shirt that stretched tight across his chest. A ripple of tattoos ran down his tanned, muscular arms. Faded jeans sat low across his narrow hips, and his thighs were so sculpted I could see their hardness through the fabric. Holy cow, this guy was ripped. And hot as Hades. I wondered in a daze whether I had ever seen a man so good looking in real life before.

"Well?" He crossed his arms and looked at me, cocking his head speculatively.

With a start, I realized I'd been staring, and that he had asked me a question. "Uh, no," I stammered. "Not lost. I just… this is my car."

One side of his mouth turned upward slightly. A jolt of electricity ran straight through me to my core. "Why's it in our parking lot?" he challenged. His brow furrowed as looked at me.

A flash of exasperation ran through me, both at Cal for putting me in this embarrassing situation, and at the mountain of muscle standing in front of me. Fighting the urge to apologize, I willed myself to keep my voice steady and firm. "I can't find the keys for it. My brother left it here for me to pick up, but the keys aren't —"

"Why did he leave it here?" he interrupted me.

Jesus, what a jerk! I fumed. Like I *wanted* to be there. "Damned if I know," I retorted, my voice coming out clipped and irritated in spite of myself. "It's not like I asked—"

"This is private property, sweetheart."

Sweetheart? Seriously? What kind of Cro-Magnon man was this, anyway? "It's not like I'm *trying* to trespass," I said sarcastically. "I just want to get my car, but—"

"You should tell your brother not to go leaving things where they don't belong."

"Look, you jerk, will you *stop* interrupting me?!" I fired back. I got out of the car and stood facing him. Well, maybe *facing* wasn't the right word. He had at least eight inches on me, eye level for me was just above his chest. I stood up as straight as I could and tried to ignore the fact that that corner of his mouth had just turned up a little more. Smug asshole, I thought. I took a deep breath. "Look," I began. "I am *trying* to get my car out of here. But my brother left it here, and I can't find the key anywhere. So until I can figure out where it is, or get hold of him, I'm stuck here. I promise you, I will get off of your very special private property just as soon as I can."

He stood there for a moment, not talking. I watched as his gaze wandered over me, sliding from my face downward, lingering on my breasts, then further down to my... oh, my... An electric thrill shot through me, and heat flooded my body. After what felt like an eternity, his eye came back up to my face and met mine. "I see. So, you've looked for the keys?"

"God... *Yes*, I've looked for them." What kind of an idiot does this misogynistic jerk think I am, anyway? "What, do you think I'm just sitting her filing my nails or something?"

"Mind if I take a look?"

"Ugh, *fine*. Be my guest," I huffed. I stepped back and let him by me, feeling the heat from his skin as he brushes close. I caught a whiff of his skin, and it smelled somehow... *impossibly* manly. But clean. Like soap and leather. It was intoxicating. I willed myself not to close my eyes and breathe in the scent of him.

He leaned into the car and checked under the mat, then above the visor. I smiled smugly. Then, looking to his left, he peered into the side pocket of the driver's side door. Reaching in, he pulled out a jingling set of keys.

He turned and stepped close to me. "These what you're looking for?" he asked, dangling them in front of my face with a lazy grin. He was only about a foot away from me now, and my face flushed hotter, partly from embarrassment that I hadn't been able to find my own keys, and partly because I suddenly found myself wondering how the combination of his rough beard and his soft lips would feel between my legs. *Whoa.*

"Yes," I said weakly. "Thank you."

"No problem." He grinned at me, a slow, lazy affair that spread across his handsome face, transforming the gruff, sexy biker's expression like we were suddenly in bed together. He was clearly enjoying that he had found what I had insisted wasn't there. Good god, he was infuriating. His gaze was boring into me, his face inches from mine now, sexy upturned lips taunting me. I bit my lip in embarrassment and looked down. He reached down with his other arm and grabbed my hand, bringing it close to him. My breath hitched at the unexpected contact. I looked up at him in confusion.

Without a word, he licked his lips slowly and dropped the keys in my hand, then closed my fingers over them. He stayed like that, his large fist around my small one, and I felt my breath grow shallow and my nipples harden with desire. I swallowed painfully and took a nervous step back, pulling my hand away from his.

His hand, now free, lifted to my face, pushing back a stray lock of my hair with a gesture that was so intimate I shivered. He drew closer to me then, and leaned in toward me until his breath was caressing my ear. "Your brother picked a mighty strange place to leave your car," he said in a low growl, his voice grown thick. "Not exactly the safest part of town." His voice dropped to a near-whisper that felt like it was singeing me from my insides out. "You like danger, honey?"

It felt like I was melting. Without even touching me, he was making me feel things that no man ever had. My lips parted involuntarily, my eyes fluttered shut for a moment. I cleared my throat and struggled to speak.

"I... he's a prospect of the motorcycle club," I stammered. "My brother. He... he took my car last night to do some club stuff and never brought it back, so he told me he'd leave it here."

The man pulled back from me for a second. His eyes lost just a hint of their fire as his expression became quizzical. "Your brother's a prospect here?" he asked, cocking his head slightly.

The drop in heat was so sudden I almost gasped. "Yes." I drew myself uncertainly up to my full height, and tried to pretend I hadn't just been in danger of bursting into flames. I swallowed again and looked him in the eye. "His name is Calvin Greenlee. Cal. Blond, tall — a little shorter than you. Good looking."

"Cal Greenlee..." He frowned for a moment, as if trying to place the name. Suddenly, his expression changed "Greenlee?" he repeated. His tone had grown strange.   Hard, all of a sudden. "Your name is Greenlee?" he asked, an edge to his voice. His eyes were boring into me now, in a way that almost frightened me. I couldn't read his expression, but it was clear I had said something that upset him.

"Yes," I said uncertainly, frowning. "Seton Greenlee." I didn't know if I should say more, so I just waited.

"Jesus Christ," he muttered under his breath. The heat of the intimate moment disappeared as quickly as it had come.

"What?" I asked. "What's wrong?"

"Nothing," he said. He took a step back, away from me. For a moment he refused to meet my eyes. "You should go. You've got your keys, you've got your car." He looked up, and his expression had become guarded, distant. "I wouldn't come back here again if I were you. This area of town isn't full of white picket fences, if you know what I mean."

And without another word, he started toward the clubhouse. I watched him, open-mouthed, as he reached the door, pulled it open, and went inside.

What the hell had just happened?

CHAPTER 4

Grey

Fuck. Fuck. Goddamn it.

There was something about her eyes. Those bright amber eyes that looked right into your soul. I saw it as soon as she looked up at me, startled, her plump, pink lips parted like they were just dying to be kissed, crazy brown curls going everywhere... There was something about her eyes that pulled me in instantly.

I couldn't believe I didn't recognize her right away. Even after all these years.

When we get prospects, the whole point is that they don't get recognized as anything other than prospects until they've proved themselves. Until then, they're just "prospect." Most of the time I don't even know their names until someone ends up slapping them with a road name that fits, but by that time they're either already patched in or just as good as.

So I had no idea that the one named Cal was fucking Calvin Greenlee. The son of the poor fucker my uncle Lawless shot because he was banging the poor fucker's old lady and got caught.

And this girl was his goddamn sister.

She looked a hell of a lot different now. Her flashing were are the same, though, even though the look of agony was gone, replaced by something deeper, clearly honed by tragedy. You could see it in her expression, she wasn't like the mostly mindless club whores that hung around us, their bodies there for the taking whenever we wanted. She had some class. And some fire. I chuckled to myself as I remembered the irritation on her face when I found the keys for her in the side pocket of her car door. No shrinking violet, this one.

I grabbed a beer from the bar and went back to my office to think. Closing the door behind me, I sat down in the swivel chair behind my desk and leaned back. I took a long, slow pull on the beer as my mind went back to my first sight of her bent over her car seat. Her tight little ass was cupped by those short shorts. Long, lean legs flexed as she bent into the search, and just the slightest shadow accentuated her inner thigh, making me imagine what would await me if I slipped a finger between the fabric and her soft skin to find the slick dampness of her.

Jesus. I was instantly hard as a rock just thinking about it. I reached down and stroked myself once through my jeans. Those perky tits straining through that tiny T-shirt, with the nicest rack I've ever seen, as she stared up at me wide-eyed and defiant. All I could think about was what it would be like to pull her out of the car and press her up against it, letting my hands do whatever they damn well pleased as she moaned and writhed against me. Goddamn, I could practically taste her, practically feel her nipples hard against my tongue as I flicked and caressed them, driving her crazy, making her thrash. I'd pull those shorts down, not giving a fuck who saw us, and lift her up onto my straining cock, taking her right there against the car as she screamed and I emptied myself inside her.

Unable to hold myself back, I unzipped and freed my aching cock. Spreading my legs, I thrust myself into my waiting hand and stroked three, four times until I came hard with a loud grunt into the waste basket. I sat back, panting, and closed my eyes with a mixture of relief and guilt.

Not guilt because she was the sister of a prospect. Fuck that.

Guilt because my family destroyed hers.

I still remembered the look in her eyes that day as she stared up at me in the crowd, hunched over the bloody corpse of her father. I had never seen a look of such desperation, such absolute loss. How her eyes picked me out, of all the other people in the crowd, I didn't know. I just knew that the look she gave me had haunted me for years. Shit, it still did from time to time. The memory of that day had stopped me from doing a few things that I might have done otherwise. As president of an MC, I couldn't afford to let my emotions get involved in my decisions. But sometimes the memory of that little girl's eyes had been something like a conscience to me. And a conscience is easier to lose than you might think.

It was the first time I had ever seen a dead body. Oh, at fifteen, I wasn't a dupe about some of the stuff the Stone Kings got up to. But my dad had taken care to shield me from the worst of it until I was older, figuring I'd find out soon enough that being a member of an outlaw motorcycle club sometimes meant doing things that weren't pleasant. I knew he always hoped I'd continue in his footsteps in the club. And hell, I could hardly imagine anything else. I'd grown up with the Stone Kings. They were my family: my uncles, brothers, cousins. Some of them were closer to me growing up than my own family was. But the day I saw my uncle Lawless kill Clayton Greenlee was the first time I'd ever thought to be ashamed of any of it.

My father, Jackson Stone, and my uncle Lucky Lawson founded the Stone Kings MC in the seventies, after my dad got back from Vietnam. Lucky was my mom's brother, and the two of them were pretty tight back then. At the time, there weren't that many motorcycle clubs in the area, so the MC's main run-ins were with the law. Eventually, the MC established itself as a fixture in Lupine, and managed to establish a working relationship with local law enforcement to keep them off the back of the club. They started doing charity runs and other things for the community, and the folks of Lupine began to accept that the club was there to stay. There hadn't been any serious brushes with the law in a while at the time of the murder. Not that the club hadn't been doing shady shit, but the police had been more than willing to look the other way in exchange for the MC keeping its nose clean in public apart from the occasional bar brawl.

My uncle Lawless changed all that. Shooting a citizen in broad daylight in the middle of main street will do that. It turned out that he had been fucking Maggie Greenlee for a while, and she had somehow gotten the impression that it was more of a relationship than just sex. When Clayton Greenlee had confronted her, she had told him that she was in love with Lawless and that he was going to take her away from dusty Lupine to some better life where she wouldn't have a drunken husband and three brats weighing her down. Clayton tracked down uncle Lawless to get his wife back, and the rest is history.

Lawless was lucky that the club had some ins with the local law enforcement. He ended up only serving three years in the state pen for Class Four felony homicide. Once he got out of prison, however, my dad and he had a falling out. Killing a member of a rival club over something like territory was one thing. But shooting a citizen over a non-club matter and making waves in the town was another. The club's relationship with Lupine was cordial, and the club wanted to keep it that way.

Uncle Lawless moved to Reno not long after that, and started a chapter there. We hadn't had a lot of contact with him since. He came up to Lupine when my dad died of heart failure three years ago, but that was the last time I'd seen him. That was probably better, as far as I was concerned. When my dad got sick, he warned me that Lawless might try to come back to the club once he was gone.

"Not everyone in the club remembers Lawless," Dad wheezed, struggling for breath without the tubes he kept pulling out of his nose in the hospital. "He's family, but he does what he wants. He hears I'm not the president anymore, he may try to come back, take over." Luckily, that hadn't happened, but it had stuck with me that my father didn't trust him. Jackson Stone was a man of few words, so when he spoke, you listened.

I was getting sick of turning all of this past history over in my head. I grunted in frustration and got up to pace. Why the fuck would a boy whose father was killed by a Stone King want to prospect with us, anyway? Goddamnit, I didn't want to know who Cal Greenlee was. I didn't want the responsibility of caring about him. I didn't want the temptation to give him special treatment because my uncle had killed his father. Or because his sister made me want to put her in my bed and fuck her senseless.

Fuck this.

I went to the door and exited the office. I needed to get outside, clear my head a bit. I wandered through the bar and out the side door to the clubhouse, then out to the back lot. Winger and Levi and a couple of the prospects were in the back by the pool tables. The one Trig had called Frankenstein was getting his ass handed to him by Levi, our Sergeant at Arms, in a game of eight ball. The other prospect, Cal, had one of the club whores named Tawny on his lap and his tongue about halfway down her throat.

"Hey, Winger," I called out. He grabbed the bottle of beer he was nursing and lumbered over to join me. Winger was a big, bald barrel of a man with a ZZ Top beard and a deep, rumbling voice that sounded like a Harley engine and scared the shit out of children and old ladies.

"Yeah, boss?" he grunted.

"The prospects look like they're havin' a little too much fun. My bike could use a wash."

He grinned. "Mine, too. Hey, prospects!" he bellowed. Frankenstein looked up from the table, cue stick in hand. Cal momentarily stopped feeling up the club whore. "Go grab some buckets. Time to wash the club's bikes."

Frankenstein simply nodded, put away the stick and walked off toward the garage. Cal seemed a little less thrilled by the idea, but he gave one of Tawny's tits a final squeeze, slapped her on the ass as she got up, and made his way over to us with a swagger.

"Sure thing, Winger," he grinned. "Where you want us to start?"

We turned and walked out toward the parking lot, Cal following at a close clip.

"You'll start with the prez's bike, over there," Winger said, pointing to my Dyna Super Glide.

Cal's eyes grew wide as he looked over at it. "Okay," he said, suddenly turning serious. I chuckled to myself. At that age, I would have had stars in my eyes looking at that bike, too. Hell, I still felt a surge of love and pride every time I got on the thing.

"And don't fuck it up," I growled, pointing a finger him. "I see one scratch on that thing when you're done, and you're dead meat."

Cal nodded, his cocky grin disappearing. "Sure thing, sir. I promise, you won't recognize it when I'm done."

"I better fucking recognize it," I spat.

"No, I meant—"

"Yeah, I got it," I cut him off. "Just fuckin' with you. Just shut up and wash my bike."

Cal broke into a raucous laugh, but then cut it off abruptly. "Seriously, though, sir. I won't let you down." He looked back over at my bike admiringly. "I've always wanted a bike like yours."

"Yeah, yeah." I stood there for a moment, and cocked my head as I gave him a good stare. Generally speaking, I didn't have much use for prospects until they'd proven themselves, but I was curious about this one in spite of myself. "You got yourself a bike yet?" I barked at him.

He nodded. "That one over there," he pointed to the far end of the parking lot. "Just got her a couple days ago," he added with pride.

I looked over at an ancient Fat Boy that he indicated. Stifling a grin, I said, "That right?"

"Yeah. I mean," he added, "It needs some work, and everything. But I'll get her runnin' like a top. She's got great bones."

"Looks to me like she's pretty big for a little shit like you."

"No, no, I can handle her just fine!" Unconsciously, Cal drew himself up to his full six feet.

I nodded soberly, suppressing the grin that was tugging at my mouth. "Good to hear it." Changing the subject, I took a couple of steps closer to him. "There was an old Mazda beater in the bar parking lot earlier today. A girl came to get it. Said you'd left it there for her."

"Yeah, that's my sister, Seton." he replied. "I borrowed her car last night for that run Winger sent us on."

"How come she came here to get it?" I asked, frowning.

He shrugged. "I was supposed to pick her up after she got off work last night — she bartends at the Cactus downtown — but the run went later than we thought, so I told her to pick it up here."

I frowned. "You took her car and you were supposed to pick her up, but you made her come all the way out here to get it? How'd she get here?"

Cal colored. "I, uh, dunno. I guess probably one of her friends drove her here."

A sudden wave of rage coursed through me, and I barely resisted the sudden urge to beat the shit out of the little punk. "That's a fucking shitty thing to do to your sister, Prospect. To any woman. This place isn't exactly the right side of the tracks."

"I'm sorry—" he began, but I cut him off. A few feet away, Winger cocked his head and looked at me with curiosity.

"You do not treat family that way." I growled, my voice rising with my anger. "You got that? You don't treat family that way. Ever." I took another step toward Cal, making sure he was very aware of the four inches I had on him. I grabbed him by the collar of his T-shirt and twisted, drawing him closer until his face was inches from mine. "This club? It's a family. These are my brothers. You never, *never*, let family down. *Nobody* becomes a Stone King who doesn't get that."

"Shit, you're right," he stammered. "I'm sorry. Really. I promise. It won't happen again." Cal backed away, raising his hands apologetically.

"You're fucking right, it won't," I said through gritted teeth. Releasing him with a push that sent him stumbling backward, I turned and walked away before I lost control. Any other prospect, I might have punched his fucking face in for less.

Then again, any other prospect and I might not have been so fucking mad that he ditched his sister.

Later on, when Cal had washed and waxed my bike to a gleaming shine, I went to find Trigger and told him I was taking off for a while. I tried to tell myself I was just going for a ride.

But I knew better. I knew I was going by the Cactus Bar to see if her car was there.

It wasn't.

But even though I tried to tell myself otherwise, I knew I'd be back.

CHAPTER 5

Seton

Two days later, I was still trying to figure out why the sexy biker I'd encountered at the MC clubhouse had reacted the way he did when I mentioned Cal was a prospect with the club. I couldn't tell by his reaction whether he knew Cal or not. But surely if there was someone who was prospecting to be a member of the club, everyone would know him?

Maybe it was that the biker was old enough to remember the story of my father's death. He looked to be in his late twenties or early thirties, in which case, he would have been too young to actually be in the club (at least, I thought so... but then again, what did I know?). But if he grew up in Lupine, maybe the name Greenlee rang a bell. Maybe he didn't know Cal's last name before I told him. But still, that didn't explain why he acted like I had leprosy the second he found out I was Cal Greenlee's sister.

I was mulling over the whole weird episode as I went for a much-needed run on Sunday morning. In a way, it was a welcome distraction from thinking about something else that had happened. I had finally screwed up my courage and broken up with Nate. Once I'd gotten my car back, I'd decided to go over to his place and pick up the few possessions that I had left over there. Unsurprisingly, he was at home, playing a video game and eating leftover pizza. He had invited me in, clearly hoping that we would be having a quick hookup. But I had somehow managed to make him realize that I wasn't kidding when I said I wanted to break up this time.

"But See, what's the problem?" he complained, his arms outstretched in a supplicating gesture as I sat on the couch next to him. "We have a great time, right? Like, I love hanging out with you and everything. I don't get it." He moved closer to me, and I caught a whiff of his stupid body spray. I realized he was about to try to wear me down, so I pulled back and put a hand on his chest.

"The problem, Nate, is that you didn't even have the decency to pick me up from work when I told you I was stranded," I pointed out.

"Look, I'm super sorry about that! I got caught up in a game with some of the guys. I didn't want to let them down," he pleaded.

Oh, brother. "Didn't want to let *them* down?" I asked incredulously. "Are you kidding me? I had to sponge a ride home with Andi — two hours later! I didn't get home until almost two a.m.!"

Nate looked away, and I have to give him credit, he blushed. "Okay, I see your point," he nodded. "That was kind of not cool." King of the understatement, Nate was. "But look, See," he said earnestly, looking back at me and fixing with his most sincere expression. "I can work on it. I can change. Come on, baby, don't be that way!"

I sighed. He looked for all the world like a hopeful puppy dog. A puppy dog with six-pack abs and gorgeous hair. But I was resolved. I shook my head. "You know, forget it. It doesn't matter. I'm sorry, Nate, but no. Look, no hard feelings, okay? It's just over. That's all."

"Yeah, okay," he said sadly, seemingly resigned. Then his eyes lit up hopefully. "But See…"

"Yeah?"

"I'm pretty sure I can get tickets to the Candy Claws concert next Friday. You wanna go?"

I realized what he was trying to do. Reel me in with a sudden gesture. Just like he always did. Looking back on our relationship, and on how many times he had done this, I suddenly felt like the biggest idiot in the world for letting him get away with it. "No, Nate," I said gently.

"I'm sure you can find someone else to go with." And I was. The random girl he was probably going to sponge the tickets off, for example.

I had to hand it to Nate, though. At least he didn't give me a hard time once he realized my mind was made up. As I left his place, even as I was sad that we had meant so little to each other, I knew it was for the best.

So, that was one guy out of my life, I thought now as I got ready for work. I wasn't really looking forward to working today, but after this I would have two days off. I was pretty pumped to just have some me-time. I was way behind on laundry, I hadn't deep-conditioned my hair in forever, and I had a library book that I wanted to finish before it was overdue. And I figured maybe Carly and I could go catch a movie or something.

That afternoon found me back behind the bar at the Cactus. I was working two p.m. until ten with Andi and a couple of the waitresses. Our boss, Wes, was there, too, trying to catch up on some bills. Wes was in his mid-forties, balding, and not fat but doughy, like someone who hardly ever did any sort of manual labor and lived on a diet of frozen pizza and Coke. He wasn't married, and as far as we knew had never been in a relationship the whole time we had known him. That didn't stop him from making crude observations about the women who came into the bar, which ones he found attractive, and which ones were "dogs." It sucked, but I mostly tried to ignore it. Jobs were kind of hard to come by in Lupine, and I needed mine.

"Look at that one," Wes was whistling under his breath as a couple of co-eds walked out the door. "Look at that ass." I had just come back from my break and was tying my apron back on.

Andi rolled her eyes and looked over at me. "Yeah, Wes, she's young enough to be your daughter. Shit, *I'm* young enough to be your daughter. Shouldn't you be leching after someone your own age? Or at least a little closer?

Wes turned away from the door and shook his head at Andi. "Andi, men are wired differently from women. We just naturally go for women with a particular hip to waist ratio," he said, as though he were a teacher lecturing a particularly dense student. "It's scientifically proven to be a biological fact. There isn't anything we can do about it."

Andi snorted. "Uh, yeah, there is. You could stop being a freaking pig whenever you see a woman younger than forty with a nice figure. Seriously, dude. Go sign up on eHarmony or whatever old people do to find love. Or at least just go jack off to Pornhub in your office and get your gross self under control."

Wes narrowed his eyes in anger. "You watch yourself, Andi." He stomped off toward the back as Andi erupted into peals of laughter.

"Jeez, Andi, that was pretty blunt," I said, worried. "Wes could fire your ass for saying stuff like that."

"Oh, please," Andi laughed. "He won't fire me. He likes staring at my tits too much."

I had to concede, Wes really did like looking at Andi's breasts. Luckily, she seemed unafraid to call him on it, and as a result, Wes never seemed to direct any sexual innuendo toward her, and seemed almost afraid of her. I knew that Andi had had a rough time growing up, and a history of some sort of sexual abuse that had gone on in her childhood with her stepfather, and that had also involved her little sister. For some women, this might have damaged them to the point where they were afraid of all men. In Andi's case, it made her determined to never let a man hurt her again. She was strong, tough, fiercely protective of all women, and seemingly unafraid of the potential danger that a sexually frustrated man with bad intentions could do.

I looked up to Andi, and the way that she took care to make herself strong and refuse to be a victim. Wes didn't frighten me exactly, but sometimes he did creep me out a little. Sometimes, after reaching up to the glass holder to put some wine glasses away, I would turn around and catch him staring at me with an expression that could only be sexual arousal. It made me uncomfortable enough to turn away, and usually that would be the end of it, but sometimes, I would look back and he'd still be staring. I wished I had Andi's guts to be able to tell him off when he did stuff like that.

I really should look for another job, I thought as I watched Wes retreat into his office. Sometimes it felt ironic that I now worked in a bar, when my dad's drinking had been the source of so much family pain. But frankly, there weren't a lot of good paying jobs in Lupine, and working at the Cactus at least gave me enough to live on and a flexible schedule. Plus, I really did like working with Andi, even though having Wes as a boss was not always a lot of fun. I had been working at the bar full-time since I'd dropped out of college after running out of money. At the time, I told myself that I was going to go back to college just as soon as I had enough money to afford another year of school, but that time had come and gone and I still hadn't reapplied.

The subject of college was one I had been trying more and more unsuccessfully not to think about lately. For a while, I had considered enrolling part-time in online classes so I work on getting my degree during my down time from work. Unfortunately, since I still hadn't decided what my major was going to be, choosing classes that wouldn't be a waste of my time and money was a challenge. One of these days, though, I knew I was going to have to get serious about figuring out what the next step was. I had saved enough money to re-enroll in college next fall if I wanted to. The trouble was, since I'd been out, I'd realized I really didn't know what I wanted to do with my life. It seemed like a waste of money to go back to school before I had that figured out.

Andi's fingers snapping in front of my face brought me out of my reverie. "Hey, girl, what's up? You fantasizing about Wes again?" She broke into another laugh as I made a disgusted face.

"Ugh, that's disgusting, Andi. For real."

"Well, I thought maybe since you and Nate are over, you were getting horny and needing some action," she grinned.

"Oh, my God," I gasped. "Can you imagine?" I shuddered. "Uh, no, I can promise you that I will *never* be that hard up."

A little while later, I had my first of many weird encounters of the day. During the Sunday afternoon lull, my deadbeat brother appeared in the doorway of the Cactus, in his Stone Kings leathers.

"Hey, See!" he called as he stepped toward the bar. He was grinning his charming "I know you're gonna forgive me" grin. I sighed. He was probably right, dammit. But damned if I was going to let him off easily.

"Hey, yourself," I replied mildly. "What are you doing here?"

"I wanted to show you something. You got a minute?"

I pursed my lips and looked over at Andi, who waved me off. "Go on, take a break. I'll cover for you. Hi, Cal!"

"Hey, Andi!" Cal said easily. His eyes ran appreciatively over her curves. "How you doin'?"

"Good," she smiled back at him. "How about you, Romeo?"

He waved back at her. "Livin' the dream, doll!"

Andi laughed and shook her head in mock disapproval. "Uh-huh, I bet. Look at you, Mister bad boy biker." Whereas Andi had never had any patience for my ex-boyfriend Nate, she always seemed to take Cal's charmer act in stride. The two of them had an easy banter that bordered on the flirtatious, and even his most exasperating behavior seemed merely to amuse her.

Cal grinned and turned back at me. "Speaking of which... come on outside! I gotta show you something!"

I rolled my eyes at Andi and followed him out into the parking lot, noting with irritation the "prospect" rocker on the back of his vest. Parked in the closest spot was a large, rough-looking Harley with tall handlebars and a windshield that he told me was called a faring. "I got her used for just five thousand dollars!" he said proudly.

"Five thousand?" I sputtered. "How the hell did you get five thousand dollars?"

"I got a loan. I'm workin' it off."

"How the hell did you get a loan?" I demanded. "As far as I know, you don't even have a job."

"I'm getting a paycheck," he countered, his voice defensive. His eyes shifted away from me. "I'm workin' for the club, so, you know..." he trailed off. Then, frowning impatiently, he looked back at me. "Come on, See, be happy for me for once! I've wanted this bike for forever."

I stared at my brother in his leathers. He looked so different from the gap-toothed little mischief-maker I remembered from when we were kids. He had the same eyes, full of sparkle and challenge, but he had filled out and grown so tall. He was at least six feet now. I hadn't noticed how muscular he had become recently. The scruff of a two day beard gave his jaw a square, rugged look. Suddenly, I felt foolish for feeling so protective of him when he was almost twice as big as I was.

I sighed. "Okay, Cal. Congratulations." I made a point of looking him in the eye. "Honestly. I mean it."

Cal seemed to relax. "Thanks, See." I smiled at him, a gesture of truce.

"So, uh..." he continued, leaning against the bike. "I also wanted to apologize for the other day. It wasn't cool of me to borrow your car and then not pick you up from work. And I should have brought the car back to you. It was the least I could have done." He looked down at the ground as he talked, the heel of his boot scuffing at the dirt.

I almost couldn't believe my ears. Cal Greenlee, apologizing for something? I hadn't heard him say he was sorry for anything since we were little kids and my mom was yelling at him for coloring on the walls or something. It was on the tip of my tongue to ask him who had put him up to it, but I stopped myself. If Cal was actually owning up for acting like a jackass, I sure as hell wasn't going to stop him. And to his credit, he did actually look contrite.

"Thank you, Cal," I said simply. "I accept your apology."

He nodded. "It won't happen again. You're my family, and I should treat you better." And then, before I could respond, he did something that almost made me faint dead away from surprise: he stood up and threw an arm around me in a brief hug. It was so unexpected and uncharacteristic that we both just stood there until eventually his arm fell away awkwardly.

While I was still trying to process what the hell had just happened, Cal cleared his throat and changed the subject.

"So, um, how's it going?"

I almost smiled at his uncomfortable attempt at making conversation, but quickly stifled it. "Not great," I said. "Nate and I broke up."

"Oh, shit. I'm sorry, See," he responded immediately. "That must, uh, be rough."

I shrugged. "It's okay. He was a lousy boyfriend, to be honest."

"Yeah," he agreed. After a moment, he continued. "You deserve someone who's nice to you. Who treats you good."

Who the hell was this Cal Greenlee? I wasn't sure I could keep up with this version without getting whiplash. "Uh, wow. Thanks, Cal," I replied, not knowing what else to say.

"I mean it," he said. "You're a good sister, and a good person," he said. After a moment of silence, where neither of us seemed to be able to think of anything to say, he took a deep breath and let it out. "Well, look," he nodded, "I better get going and let you get back to work." He stepped over to the motorcycle and swung his leg over it. "Maybe we could get together next week some time for lunch," he offered.

I smiled. "I'd like that." Whether the actual lunch date ever really happened or not, it was nice that he had even thought of it.

He nodded at me and gave me a two-fingered wave, then started his bike and rolled out of the parking lot. I listened to the low rumble of the Harley recede into the distance as I thought to myself that I could never have predicted that scene in a million years.

The rest of the afternoon seemed to pass at a snail's pace. Even with Andi to keep me company, Sundays were always slow, and I was really antsy to finish my shift and start my "weekend." We passed the time by chatting about her latest boy toy, a tattoo artist who was apparently tattooed "down there." We had a bit of a bump during dinner, but by the time eight o'clock rolled around, there was only one couple in the bar.

It was time for my second break around 8:15, so I left the bar for the back hallway, intending to go out the back door and go sit outside on the old picnic table that was our makeshift break room. As I rounded a corner, I literally ran into Wes as he came out of his office. I startled at the unexpected contact, his arm brushing up against my breasts. I stepped back immediately. "Whoa, sorry," I laughed.

"If you wanted to make a pass at me, you should have just asked," Wes replied in a tone that was meant to be joking, but felt a little off.

"Ha, funny," I replied.

"Andi got things under control out front?" Almost imperceptibly, he stepped closer to me. His face reddened, and I could hear his rapid breathing.

"Um, yeah, I was just going out back to take a break," I said. I tried to move back to increase the distance between us, but the corridor was narrow and I couldn't move without it being obvious that I was trying to get away from him. Nervously, I nodded toward the back door. "I could use a little air."

"You want some company?" he asked. His lower lip glistened with saliva under the fluorescent light.

"Um, no thanks," I said, shaking my head. In desperation, I ducked around him and moved quickly down the hall. "I'm good."

I exited the building and quickly shut the door after me. Outside, I tried to slow my breathing and the sudden hammering of my heart. Wes had always been a little creepy, but he had never tried anything like this. Thankfully, he didn't come outside after me. I spent my break walking around the back perimeter of the property, almost pacing, trying to talk myself down. By the time my fifteen minutes were up, I had calmed myself down to the point where I was almost questioning whether what I thought had happened had happened.

I went back into the bar, walking quickly by the office door, which was closed. A few minutes after I resumed working, Wes came out front. "Seton, clock out and go home," he barked. "Andi, you can handle the rest of the night, can't you?"

Andi snorted. "If I can't handle *this*, then there's something wrong," she said, looking around the empty bar.

Moving quickly so as to avoid another possible hallway encounter with Wes, I went in the back and grabbed my purse. Back in the bar, I avoided Wes's eyes and waved goodbye to Andi, who was arguing with him about discontinuing a liqueur.

Out in the parking lot, the evening light was just beginning to change as the sun began its descent downward. I breathed in deeply and then let it out again, relieved to be get some distance from the strangeness of what had just happened, and happy at the prospect of two entire days of freedom.

There, as I turned toward where my car was parked, was my third weird encounter of the day. I jumped and let out a tiny shriek of surprise.

Sitting on his motorcycle, next to my car, was the biker from two days ago.

CHAPTER 6

Grey

This was the last thing I should be doing. I knew it damn well. And I knew just as well that I was gonna do it anyway.

Ever since that girl sped out of the club's parking lot a couple of days ago, I'd had a damn hard-on for her that just wouldn't seem to go away. Jesus, I'd been jacking off multiple times a day just to try to keep my mind off of her. I hardly ever jacked off. I didn't have to. It wasn't like I was hard up for women; hell, most of the time I had my choice of pussy whenever and wherever I wanted. But I just kept picturing her eyes flashing at me as she talked, the fire in her, her perfect tight little ass...

In the past few days I had imagined taking her every way I could think of. I'd thought about yanking off her shorts and sliding my fingers between her legs to find her wetness, waiting as her breath hitched and she started to moan for me, louder and louder, writhing against my hand, begging me to take her further. I'd imagined my tongue buried between her legs, tasting her, licking and sucking at her until she screamed my name. I'd plunged my cock deep inside her as she gripped my arms desperately thrashing against me, meeting me thrust for thrust until I emptied myself deep inside her...

My cock was rock hard just thinking about it, and I was shifting uncomfortably on the seat of the bike when suddenly the door to the bar opened and there she was. She looked startled to see me, but after stopping in her tracks for a moment, she set her shoulders and walked toward me. She was wearing this little pair of black shorts that showed off her legs and a tight pink T-shirt that showed off the curve of her tits. Her hair was pulled back in a pony tail that I instantly wanted to wrap around my hand so I could pull her head back and crush my mouth down on hers.

I'd been sitting there beside her car for the better part of an hour, smoking and waiting for her to come out. Trying not to ask myself any questions about why the hell I was there in the first place. Now here she was, and damned if I had the first idea what I was going to say or do that wouldn't make her run the fuck away from me.

Whatever her reaction was at seeing me there, she recovered quickly. She walked up to me and stopped about six feet away, a challenge in her eyes. She leaned against her car and faced me.

"You lost?" she asked with a smirk.

"Nope, I'm not lost." I took a drag of my smoke. "I know exactly where I am."

"Why's your bike in this parking lot? This is private property," she shot back. I realized the game she was playing then. I decided to play along.

"Your brother leave your car in another bar parking lot?"

She laughed, genuinely amused. The sound took me by surprise; it was unguarded, bubbly and unrestrained. After the tension of our first encounter, hearing her laugh like that felt strangely intimate, like I was glimpsing part of her that she didn't give out to just anyone. It made my dick jump.

It made me want to hear it again.

"No," she replied as her laughter faded. "I work here. See?" She pointed to the cactus logo on the T-shirt she was wearing, a gesture that just gave me an excuse to look at her fucking perfect tits. Which I did. For a while.

"Hey, caveman. I'm up here."

I drag my eyes back up to her face. "You're the one that just asked me to look at your breasts. I was just being agreeable," I pointed out.

Her mouth opened slightly in surprise, and then her skin began to flush pink. "I did *not!*" she protested, her voice rising slightly. Her breathing started to speed up a little. She stood there, eyes flashing in irritation. There was just something about her that made me want to rile her up some more.

A stray lock of hair had fallen into her face, and she blew it away in frustration. "So, why *are* you here, anyway? Are you just making it a special point to track me down just to irritate me?"

I chuckled. "I didn't have to track you down. Your car is pretty noticeable." I nodded at the dent in the side panel.

"So you're expecting me to believe that you just happened to notice my car here and decided to stop by for a chat?"

"Maybe," I said. "That so hard to believe?"

She rolled her eyes in exasperation. "Last time I saw you, you were telling me to get the hell off your property."

I stood up and walked over to her until I was close enough to see the flush of her skin. "I wasn't telling you to get off my property," I said, stepping closer until I was almost pressing against her. "I was telling you you should be careful in a part of town you don't know."

She looked up at me, her face defiant. "Is that so?" she breathed.

"Yes. That's so." I affirmed. Nervously, she caught her lower lip in her teeth, and my dick surged against my zipper. I was so hard I could barely stand it. Her breasts were rising and falling rapidly, and for a second, her eyes flickered closed. I could tell I was getting to her as much as she was getting to me. "One minute you think you're safe, and then the next… you're in over your head." I leaned in close, my mouth inches from hers, and her lips parted instinctively. I chuckled, and she drew back, embarrassed. "Admit it, babe," I said. "You're in over your head."

She inhaled sharply, ready to protest that I was full of shit, but I couldn't take it anymore. My mouth came crashing down on hers, my hand fisting in her hair as I leaned her against the car. She moaned into my mouth, her lips opening as my insistent tongue took possession of hers. Her hands went to my arms and she pulled me against her, kissing me back.

Finally kissing her, finally touching her after thinking about nothing else for days practically drove me crazy with need. Leaning against the car, I pressed my full length against her and reached down, cupping her ass with my hands. I lifted her up slightly so that she was pressed against me, her softness meeting the hardness of my need. A sharp moan of desire ripped through her at the contact and her hips thrust forward to meet me, her body taking over. Her lips broke apart from mine as she threw her head backward, gasping, "Oh…God…"

"You see what kind of danger you could get into?" I murmured against her ear, and felt her shiver in response. "You gotta be careful talking to strangers."

"Name," she gasped.

"What?" I groaned.

"I don't know your name," she said breathlessly.

"Greyson Stone," I growled.

She pulled her head back and looked at me. Biting her lip, she cocked her head and gave me a slight, teasing smile. "There," she panted. "Now we're not strangers."

I laughed, and our mouths found each other again in a rough, desperate kiss. I slid one of my hands up to the small of her back, holding her hard against me. She lifted her arms to my neck and pulled my mouth toward her, and I felt her breasts rising and falling as her breath came in a heavy, rapid rhythm. I thought about pulling her onto the hood of the car and just taking her right there, but for some reason I wanted to take my time with this one. So instead, I slid my other hand in between us and flicked open the button on her shorts.

Slowly, slowly, I unzipped them, then slid my hand further down the front, above the fabric of her panties. She gasped and started to pull back, but I held her fast. It was a supreme effort of will to go slow, but I skimmed the surface of her panties as lightly as I could as I lightened the touch of my kiss, as well, to make her come to me. After a moment, her moans turned to a whimper of frustration as she started to thrust her hips toward my hand. I chuckled and thought, *I've got her.*

As I continued to fondle and tease her, I found myself wondering what color her panties were. *I'll find out*, I promised myself. For now, I continued to lightly caress her hardening nub through the fabric as I listened to her whimpers grow louder.

When I sensed her frustration begin to build to the breaking point, I slipped a finger inside to find the warm wetness of her. She gasped, and her hold on my neck tightened. She was tensed as taut as a drum, wanting release so badly, but I could feel from the rigidness of her body that she was trying to keep her last shreds of composure. But composure wasn't what I wanted from her.

"Tell me what you want," I growled into her ear. She let out a soft whine but said nothing. "Tell me," I repeated. "Tell me what you want me to do to you."

Ducking her head, she whispered something so quietly I had to tell her to say it again. "Make me come," she repeated breathlessly. I smiled in satisfaction. *Good.* I've never forced a woman to do anything in my life, and I sure as hell wasn't gonna start now. She was going to tell me exactly how much she wanted what I do to her.

I pulled my hand away momentarily, just to tease her, and she whimpered and clung to me. "Please..." she whispered. "Oh, please..."

My cock strained against the zipper of my jeans as she begged me to make her come. Jesus fuck, I was gonna blow in my fucking pants if I wasn't careful. "Someday," I growled into her ear as my fingers found her again, one sliding inside her as I resumed stroking her clit. "Someday, I'm gonna bury my face in between those legs and lick your pussy until you come all over my face. I'm gonna make you scream so loud your throat will be raw for days. And then I'm gonna fuck you like you've never been fucked before. You know it's gonna happen. You want that, don't you?"

"Oh, God," she moaned, and threw her head back. She was so close, and I was tempted to keep her there indefinitely, but she was so fucking sexy like that that I just wanted to see her come. I swirled my wet finger around her desperate nub one more time and then lightly pinched and stroked her between my thumb and middle finger, and just like that she flew over the edge. My lips crashed down on hers as she rode the wave of her orgasm, screaming into my mouth as she writhed and shuddered.

It was the best goddamn feeling in the world. Maybe even better than coming.

As I waited for her to quiet, I held her against the car until her breathing began to slow. When she finally opened her eyes and looked at me, they were dark and wide with passion. She cut a look toward the bar and the empty parking lot. "I can't believe we just did that," she whispered.

I laughed and smoothed back a lock of her hair. There was just something about this girl. This combination of innocent and saucy. "Believe it. I was a witness," I grinned.

She blushed then, and looked down. She was embarrassed. She was fucking embarrassed, and it was the most gorgeous thing I've ever seen. "A very *willing* witness," I corrected. "That was hot."

A giggle burst out of her, half-hysterical. "I've just… never, well… done anything like that," she admitted.

"Seems like it was high time you did," I remarked, raising an eyebrow.

"I meant… I mean, I've done… ugh," she frowned. I was rewarded with another blush. "I mean… with basically a stranger, and in public."

"There's no one around," I said dismissively, looking around. "And besides, you yourself said I'm not a stranger now." I winked at her.

She smiled shyly. It was cute, considering I'd just had my hand down her pants and made her come. "You said your name was Greyson?" she asked.

"Grey. Greyson Stone."

"And… you're a member of the Stone Kings." Her smile was fading now.

"Yeah." No reason to tell her any more than necessary.

"So… you know my brother Cal."

"Yeah. I do."

She seemed to be on the verge of saying something else, but apparently thought better of it. "So, what does Cal have to do to join the club?"

"Pretty much anything the club asks him to do. Wash our bikes. Go buy us beer." I skip some of the rougher stuff. "Basically, prove loyalty and respect to the club. Show responsibility."

She laughed. "Cal's not long on responsibility."

I frowned. "We'll see. Prospects don't make it very far unless they do what they say they're gonna do."

She seemed to visibly relax as I said this. *Huh.* I guessed it wasn't too surprising that a sister wouldn't be exactly thrilled about her brother joining a one-percenter club, but this was the first time I'd really thought about it directly.

"Seton," I mused. "That's an unusual name."

"Most people call me See. It's my mom's maiden name," she explained. She seemed happy to change the subject. "Not that I know why my mom named me after her family. I only met my mom's parents once. She certainly didn't seem to have much of an attachment to them."

I nodded, taking in what she said. "Your mom still around?"

She scoffed. "'Around' is up for debate. She's still alive, yes. She lives in Scottsdale. With her boyfriend." She paused, then continued. "My dad's dead."

I took a deep breath. What should I say to that? That I knew? That I was there when it happened? That my uncle had been the one to do it? There was too much there, it seemed. Too much weight to it.

So I took the fucking coward's way out.

"I'm sorry," I murmured. "Do you have any siblings other than Cal?"

"Another brother," she replied. "Reed. The oldest. I think he's out in Denver somewhere."

I took note of the way she said it. "Sounds like your family isn't all that close."

"Nope," she replied, her tone angry, brusque. Something shifted between us, and suddenly the temperature seemed to drop ten degrees. Abruptly, she moved a step away from the car — away from me —

and looked awkwardly at the ground. "Um. I think I should be going now."

I couldn't think of anything else to say, so I let her take the lead.

"Yeah. Okay," I nodded. She reached for the handle of her car door like she suddenly realized she was late for an appointment.

"Um. Bye," she said, refusing to look at me.

I watched her drive away.

"Bye," I said.

CHAPTER 7

Seton

I barely slept that night.

When I got home from my encounter with Greyson Stone, Carly was there. She seemed to realize that there was something up with me, because she kept looking at me out of the corner of her eyes and trying not to let me notice. I knew I was acting nervous and weird, and I could tell I still had the flush of sex in my face, just from the way I felt. When Carly had asked me how my day had gone, I just managed to make her believe that I was acting strange because I was freaked out about Wes cornering me alone in the hallway. Which, to be honest, I was still freaked out about. But that's not what was on my mind as I got ready for bed.

I was thinking about Greyson Stone, and how he had almost driven me out of my mind with just his hand.

I lay in bed, staring at the ceiling for what felt like hours. I couldn't stop thinking about him, and what he'd done to me. Belatedly, I realized I'd been so discombobulated by the way he had teased and tormented me that I hadn't even noticed he hadn't finished himself. He had made it all about me, making me his with just a whisper and a touch. Had he not wanted me? I worried, blushing at how wanton I'd been, letting basically a stranger do whatever he pleased with my body. But the memory of his lips, soft but hard, and the gruff brush of his beard against my skin sent a rush of heat coursing through my body, and I thought back to what he had whispered in my ear right before he had made me come:

"Someday, I'm gonna bury my face in between those legs and lick your pussy until you come all over my face. I'm gonna make you scream so loud your throat will be raw for days. And then I'm gonna fuck you like you've never been fucked before. You know it's gonna happen. You want that, don't you?"

Oh, God, yes. I wanted that.

And just like that, even though Grey had made me come harder than I ever had before, the thought of what he had promised me at that moment made me ache with an unbearable need to be released. I lay in bed, my body on fire, throbbing for his touch, until finally I reached under the covers and brought myself to orgasm, whispering his name as I came. Finally, I was able to fall into a fitful sleep, where I had dreams of him between my legs.

The next morning, I was feeling unsettled but better. In the light of day, what had happened between Gray and me in the parking lot felt more like a dream than reality. Even so, I found that I couldn't quite get him out of my mind. Carly had left early for a training class at the salon where she worked, so I was on my own for the day. The prospect of two days without any routine, which had sounded so attractive to me yesterday, now felt like torture. So, I decided to do what I always do when I'm feeling jittery or on edge.

I cook.

I spent the morning distracting myself from thinking about Grey by dreaming up different dishes I'd like to try, and making a shopping list. After a quick run to the store, I came back and cleared the kitchen counters in preparation for a long day of cooking. I picked some rhubarb from the tiny patch of land I'd managed to commandeer in the side yard, and with the strawberries I'd bought at the supermarket, I set out to make a strawberry-rhubarb pie. Once I had the pie in the oven, I started preparations to make a new recipe for homemade ravioli with arugula and pancetta. I'd found the recipe online a few weeks earlier and hadn't yet had the time to try it. The recipe involved making the pasta from scratch, which was just the kind of meditative work I was looking for.

I'd been in the kitchen for a couple of hours when I got a text from Cal.

Hey wats up

Immediately suspicious that he was going to ask me for a favor, I texted back:

Not much. You?

Just wondering how u were doing. u want to go get dinner or something?

Surprised but pleased, I thought for a second and then wrote him a reply.

I'm cooking ravioli and strawberry-rhubarb pie. Want to come over here for dinner?

A few seconds later I got this:

That sounds great! When?

I replied:

Come over whenever you want.

The response was immediate:

Cool ill be there in an hour

I set down my phone, trying to wipe the floury fingerprints from the screen, and turned back to my work, humming. I thought back to how I had learned to cook in the first place. When Reed had left home, my mom had pretty much abandoned all pretense of taking care of Cal and me. After a few months of existing on microwave burritos and frozen pizza, I had taken on the task of making us food so we wouldn't starve to death. I had started with simple things that took ingredients that we were likely to have in our poorly stocked kitchen: quesadillas, grilled cheese sandwiches, spaghetti. Eventually, as I got older and earning some money babysitting, I would sometimes use my allowance to buy more exotic ingredients. I liked the peaceful meditativeness of cooking. I liked that it felt like I was in control when I was in the kitchen. And if something didn't turn out, I was the one who had made the mistake — which meant that I could learn how to correct it.

I hadn't been cooking much lately, so this impromptu time in the kitchen felt especially precious to me now. I resolved not to let so long go before I spent an afternoon cooking again.

A little over an hour later, the low sound of a motorcycle engine approached. I suppressed my irritation at the thought of Cal making such an irresponsible purchase, and washed my hands so I could go get the door. I got to the door and opened it just as he was about to ring the bell.

Cal was standing there in a clean white T-shirt and his leathers, and held a six pack of beer in his left hand.

I tried not to show my shock. This was the first time I could ever remember him not showing up to my place empty handed. Normally, Cal took. He didn't give.

"Hey, sis!" He said with a grin. He opened the screen door and gave me a quick hug as he passed through. "I hope this goes with ravioli," he said, holding up the six pack.

"Beer goes with anything," I assured him. "Go on through to the kitchen."

I followed him through the living room and watched as he went to the refrigerator to put the beer in. He took a beer out and offered it to me. Another first: the Cal I knew should have just taken one for himself and thrown the rest in the fridge.

"Thanks," I said dumbly as I took the bottle from him. He nodded and took a second one out of the pack before putting the rest in the fridge.

Cal sat at the kitchen table as I worked on dinner, sipping his beer and telling me funny stories about what he'd been doing since I'd last seen him. I decided to take a cue from his new-found thoughtfulness and put him to work on making a salad.

"Here," I said, handing him a head of Romaine lettuce. "Wash this, and then tear off the leaves and throw them in the salad spinner."

"Come on, See, I don't know how to do this stuff!" he complained.

"Sure you do," I replied, waving him off. "Wash. Tear off leaves. Tear them into a size that's easy enough to eat with a fork. Throw in salad spinner. Spin. If you can figure out the mechanics of a motorcycle, you can do this."

"Fine," he grumbled, but he took the lettuce from me and went to the sink. He even did a halfway decent job of it. I had him grate some parmigiano to go on top of the salad and the pasta, and by that time, I was more or less finished with the rest of the meal.

Cal set the table while I plated the food and brought it in. Cal got himself a second beer, and without pretense dug into the pasta. "Oh my God," he groaned as he chewed. "Damn, See, I'd forgotten what a good cook you are."

"Thanks," I smiled, and loaded up my fork. "I'm glad you like it."

"It's freaking fantastic," he enthused, taking another bite. "You know, you really should cook for a living. You'd be a great chef."

"I don't know about that," I protested, but I smiled happily. It was nice to be appreciated. And if I did say so myself, the ravioli was pretty damn good.

We ate in silence for a couple of minutes, during which time I found my thoughts turning back to Grey, and the Stone Kings.

"So…" I asked. "Things are good with you, it sounds like."

"Yeah, great," he nodded. "I mean, I'm pretty busy with the MC, but I like that, you know?"

"What… what sort of stuff do you do with them?" I asked, trying to keep my tone light.

Cal looked at me briefly, and then back down to his plate. "Uh, actually, See… I can't really talk about it. See, that's kind of one of the things. Loyalty to the club is really important, and that involves keeping club business to ourselves."

I frowned. "It's not, like, anything illegal, is it?"

Cal looked back up at me. "Look, See, I don't want to talk about it. No offense. But I'm not going to."

I didn't know what to make of that. But Cal seemed pretty resolute, so I figured that pushing him on it wouldn't get me anywhere, anyway. So, I tried another angle.

"What are the other members of the club like?"

"Tough," he admitted. "Like, 'don't fuck with me' tough. These guys don't take shit from anyone. But they're like a family. A brotherhood." His tone grew enthusiastic. "The president, Grey, he comes off as really hard, and he can be pretty rough on the prospects. But I think underneath he's a really good guy. The rest of the brothers in the club seem to really respect him."

Cal kept talking, but I didn't hear much after that. My mind was in a daze. Grey was the president of the Stone Kings? I had only barely been able to get my mind around the fact that the man who had leaned me up against my car and made me scream with pleasure was a member of a biker gang… but the *president*?

What did the president of an MC even do?

Then it hit me. The man who had done things to me I didn't even think were possible wasn't just some random member of the Stone Kings. He was the *head* of the Stone Kings. And although he was clearly too young to have been involved with my father's death, he might know the person who killed him. Maybe even well.

Grey Stone was my enemy. Why didn't I feel the hatred that I should? My stomach roiled in confusion and I put down my fork, my appetite suddenly gone.

Cal had continued to talk as my thoughts spun out of control, but he eventually noticed that I didn't seem to be paying much attention. "You're awfully quiet all of a sudden, See," he remarked. "Anything wrong?"

I didn't trust myself to speak, so I choked out the only response I could. "I'm fine."

Cal must have interpreted my silence as worry. "See," he began, "it's okay. Really. Nothing bad's gonna happen to me. The club isn't what you think it is."

"Isn't it?" I asked sharply.

Cal looked down uncomfortably. "Well, I mean… they're not choir boys. But the club protects its own. And they do a lot of good in the community. Silent auctions, bike runs for charity…"

"Stop," I interrupt him. "Just, stop."

He stopped talking, his brow furrowing in frustration.

I sat still for a moment, willing myself to change the subject. But I couldn't stop myself from asking the question I knew he wouldn't want to hear.

"Cal, doesn't it bother you at all that a Stone King killed our father?" I asked quietly.

Cal shook his head. "I don't wanna talk about that, See."

"What? Why the hell not?" I asked, my voice rising. "How can you possibly not have a problem with that? I don't understand how you think it's just fine that a club you are prospecting with is responsible for our father's death!"

"Stop it!" Cal yelled. He shook his head angrily. "Seton, there's stuff you don't know. Stuff Mom told me. Dad brought it on himself. He never should have gone after a club member. Dad was nothing but a drunk, anyway."

It was as though he'd dropped a bomb right in the middle of the room. "How *dare* you talk about our father that way!" I shouted, my eyes filling with furious tears.

"See—" Cal began.

"No!" I yelled. I slammed my fist down on the table. "Get out, Cal! Get out now!"

Cal stood and watched helplessly as I put my head down on the table and sobbed. I couldn't believe that my brother thought of our father as nothing but a useless drunk. Cal had been so young when Daddy died, he barely remembered him, I knew. Just like I knew instinctively that my mother had reduced him in Cal's eyes to nothing but a sad caricature. But it didn't matter that I knew it wasn't true. I couldn't take it. My heart couldn't take it.

Cal tried to touch me once, on the shoulder, but I angrily pushed him away. Eventually, I heard him walk slowly toward the door and leave, shutting the screen quietly behind him.

I couldn't bear for Cal to be part of the Stone Kings MC. I just couldn't.

I would do anything to stop him.

Even if it meant confronting Greyson Stone.

CHAPTER 8

Grey

"Okay, meeting called to order." I banged the gavel once.

The raucous chatter around the table subsided, as one by one, my brothers settled in and turned to look at me.

"We all know what we're here to talk about," I said as I looked around the table. "It's time to find out who's behind Hammer's death." A couple of the members nodded. "So. Talk."

To my right, Trig spoke up. "Gotta be the Cannibals." A murmur of assent went around the table.

"What's the motive?" I shot back. I knew my VP, and we called him Trigger for a reason. He was a shoot first, ask questions later type. His instincts were usually good, but there were still a lot of questions that were unanswered. I wanted to be one hundred percent goddamn sure before we planned our payback.

"Who else could it be?" Levi, my Sergeant at Arms, said. His brow was furrowed in a murderous glower. Levi had a slow burn, but once he was mad, he was a powder keg. I could see it in his eyes that the burn had begun.

"If it was the Cannibals, why the hell haven't they taken credit for it?" I challenged him. "It doesn't make any sense that they'd do something like this unless they wanted us to know it was them."

"Coulda been lots of people," Sag agreed. "Undercover cop?"

"Nah, that makes no sense," I countered. "We got friends in the force. Doesn't make sense we wouldn't have heard something by now, if something was going down."

"The Cannibals haven't been a problem for a long time," Repo called from further down the table. "We got an understanding with them. They stay in their territory, we stay in ours. Everything's copasetic."

"Yeah, but they got a new prez," Trigger said, his dark eyes flashing under his furrowed brows. "And we don't know much about him other than he used to be their sergeant at arms."

"That's not enough," I countered. "We need to know more before we start a war with the Cannibals over this."

"Too bad the only guy who could have told us more ran away from the scene like a fucking pussy," Levi said in disgust. Angry mutters circled the table. Jethro's betrayal would rankle the brothers for a long time.

"So, how do we find out more?" Sag asked the table.

"We do something provocative," Trigger replied. "See how hard they bite."

I chewed on this for a minute. "What you got in mind?"

Trigger squinted for a moment in thought. "We take a little Sunday drive into their territory. See how much of a reaction we get."

"Seems risky," Sag countered.

"Not if there's nothing going on," Trigger said. "We just get our hands slapped. No worries at all." He spread his hands wide and smiled.

"It's not a bad idea," I admitted. "Could tell us a lot." I looked at Trigger. "Since it's your idea, you go. But you need to keep your hair trigger in check, brother. This is reconnaissance, nothing more. No escalation. Make this look like a simple joyride, even if they'll know it isn't."

"How about if I take the prospects along?" Trigger suggested. "The Cannibals would never expect us to bring prospects on a kill mission."

The prospects. It was a good idea. Really good. Bringing the prospects along would de-escalate a possible confrontation as long as the Cannibals didn't have specific orders about us. And it would be good training for the prospects, as well as a chance for Trigger to see how they acted in a tense situation.

But all I could see was Seton's face if something went wrong and Cal got hurt.

Goddamn it. No. No. I couldn't let decisions about the club be influenced by some girl with good tits and a hot ass I was itching to fuck. It wasn't good for anybody if I did that. I had a responsibility to the Stone Kings. My brothers. I couldn't let my dick make my choices for me.

I turned and nodded at Trigger. "Good idea. Take the prospects with you. And..." I looked around the room. "Take Repo, too." Repo was my road captain. He was ace at keeping his eyes open.

Trigger looked at Repo and lifted his chin in acknowledgement. "You ready to go now?"

Repo nodded once. "Yup. Let's go round up the prospects."

"Okay," I said. "Any other business?" The table was quiet.

"Move to adjourn," Trigger said.

"Second," Repo added.

I banged the gavel. One by one, the brothers began to file out of the room, talking quietly among themselves.

Levi came up to us and looked at Trigger. "You guys are sitting ducks if the Cannibals are responsible for this. You should take me with you."

I tried to shrug off the possibility. "Nah. They wouldn't bother going after prospects if they were serious. They'd be going after bigger guns. But they might do something to scare the shit out of them. This is good intel. And it's also a good way to find out if the prospects have enough mettle to be Stone Kings."

Levi's brow creased into a frustrated frown, but he nodded. "Okay," he said simply.

I turned to Trigger and glanced at Repo, who had come up beside us. "You good, brothers?"

"Yeah," Repo said. "We're good."

"All right. Give me an update as soon as you're back."

I watched them go, then closed the door to the chapel, and tried to get Seton Greenlee's face out of my thoughts.

It had been over a week since I'd seen her. Not that I was counting or anything.

I'd been trying to keep my distance. Keeping myself as busy as possible so I wouldn't be tempted to go see her again. She had left so abruptly that night, I wanted to give her space.

But as much as I had tried to put her out of my mind, I just kept coming back to her. Her flashing eyes as she sparred with me. Her crazy mixture of innocence and red-hot sexiness. The way her cheeks and neck flushed when she was turned on. The little sounds she made when she wanted more. The way she threw back her head and moaned right before she came.

Fuck. I was hard as a rock just thinking about it all.

As I watched her drive away that night, I was already thinking about how to see her again. But as the days went by, I started to realize it just wasn't in the cards. I never should have gone to see her in the first place. I wasn't even sure what the hell had possessed me to.

Sure, she was gorgeous, and hot as fucking hell. But I'd never been short on pussy, and I'd never felt any one woman was worth getting all tangled up for. I sure as hell wasn't relationship material. Seton was. She wasn't my type at all. She was smart. She was classy. She had a future. She deserved better than me. She was exactly the opposite of the club whores that I usually resorted to in order to satisfy my sexual whims. Sex-wise, I had always specifically done everything I could to avoid exactly the situation I found myself in.

And now, here I was, unable to get a woman out of my mind. I couldn't whether to protect her, get rid of her, or fuck her senseless.

I was turning around these three possibilities in my head, just as I had been doing for days, when a soft knock on the closed door of the chapel interrupted me.

"Hey, boss?" Tammy called. She opened the door and poked her head in timidly. "There's uh, someone to see you out in front."

I frowned. "Who is it?"

Her expression was perplexed. "Uh, I'm not sure. It's a woman."

I walked out front to see Seton Greenlee standing by the bar.

CHAPTER 9

Seton

I heard his footsteps coming down the hall before I saw him. The peroxide-blonde bartender who had gone back to get him reappeared, her eyes flicking momentarily toward me and then looking away nervously. Behind her, Grey emerged.

He was wearing a dark gray T-shirt that accentuated the muscles in his chest and arms, and worn, faded jeans that looked so soft I wanted to touch them. Standing there watching the muscled fluidity of his movements sent my mind back to the last time I'd seen him, to what he had done to me, and I felt my face flush. *Dammit.* I stood up taller, squaring my shoulders. I couldn't let myself think about that now.

Grey stopped about three feet in front of me. His eyes raked lazily down and then up my body, stopping occasionally to linger a second or two too long. "To what do I owe the pleasure, sweetheart?" he murmured, his lips turning up in a sexy, infuriating half-grin.

"I need to talk to you," I said coldly.

"You're talking already," he observed, his grin getting a little wider.

"In private," I said angrily through clenched teeth. I nodded my head toward the blond bartender, who was pretending not to listen to our conversation.

Grey chuckled and held up his hands in a mocking gesture of surrender. "Okay, whatever you need, sweetheart."

"And don't call me sweetheart."

"Right this way, sugar," he replied without skipping a beat. Turning, he motioned for me to follow him down the dark hallway. At the end of the corridor, he pushed open a door and motioned for me to step inside. Only once he had followed me in and closed the door did I realize that maybe it hadn't been the best decision to ask to be alone with him.

"So." Grey leaned against his desk and crossed his arms. He cocked his head at me with that perpetually amused smirk on his face. "What did you want to 'talk' to me about?" His mocking tone implied that I had other motives. I was instantly furious with him for suggesting that I was here because of what had happened between us last time, but told myself to keep my cool and not let him goad me.

"You didn't tell me you were the club president," I accused him.

"You didn't ask me." Grey pointed out.

"Doesn't that seem like the kind of thing you would have told me?"

"I don't see why," he shrugged. "You're not in the club."

"But my *brother* is."

"So what?" he challenged.

"So *what*?!" I cried. "What the hell is that supposed to mean?"

"I don't see what that has to do with anything," Grey said coolly. "His life is his life. Your life is yours."

"Grey, he's my brother. He's practically my only family," I pleaded.

"He's a consenting adult." His voice was a statement not a question. I colored.

"I know. I know," I said. Suddenly, my emotions threatened to overcome me and I had to fight to blink back angry, frustrated tears.

Grey's tone softened. "So... what are you saying?" he asked more gently.

I cleared my throat and willed my voice not to crack. "I came to ask you a favor," I said, more loudly than I had intended.

His half-smile returned. "I thought you weren't here about that."

"Goddamnit, stop being so infuriating! I'm serious!" I cried.

He made a half-effort to stop smiling, but his eyes still twinkled with merriment. "Okay. What's the favor?"

"I want you to…" I stumbled over the wording. "Un-prospect Cal."

A low laugh came rumbling from deep in his throat. "You want me to do what?"

"Un-prospect him," I repeated more firmly. "Whatever it's called. I want you to refuse to let him into the club."

"Seton," Grey began. The twinkle in his eyes disappeared. "I'm not gonna do that."

"What? Why?" I demanded, incredulous. "You can do it, right? You're the president. You can do anything."

"I can. I could. But I won't." His expression was set, his jaw firm.

"Why not?" I cried. "Why can't you do this?" I tried not to say it, but I couldn't stop myself. "For me?"

He gave me a long, penetrating look, then shook his head. "I'm not going to mix up the club's business and… this," he said. "They need to be kept separate. That's my job as president: to keep my personal life from affecting decisions about the club."

"Grey, please," I begged. "He's too young. He's only nineteen."

"I was seventeen when I prospected," he remarked with a smirk.

"That's different. You're… he's…" I stammered.

"Not trash?" he smirked, a challenge in his eye.

"That's… no! That's not what I meant!"

"What did you mean, then?" he growled.

"Just that…" I struggled to find the words. "He's not tough enough."

"That's for the club to decide," he retorted. "That's what prospecting is about."

I tried again. "Look, he's… he's too immature. He's never thad to handle anything really tough in his life. He doesn't have what it takes to do this." I looked at him. "Please."

"He's got to grow up sometime," Grey said.

"Not this way."

"Oh for fuck's sake, don't act like his mom," he growled.

"If I acted like his mom, I wouldn't give a shit," I shot back.

The words came out of my mouth without me wanting them to. I stomped my foot in exasperation. He had no right to know about our personal family history. He knew too much already.

Grey's expression changed, to something I couldn't quite read. He stood up slowly, and came toward me until he was standing only inches away. I should have moved back, but I didn't.

"Seton," he said softly. His hand came up and cupped my chin. "I'm sorry." He paused for a moment, then continued. "I know about your dad. That he was killed. That it was a Stone King who did it."

I froze. I did not want to have this conversation. Not with Grey. Not with anyone.

"I didn't know who Cal was when he started hanging around," he continued. "That he was Clayton Greenlee's son. I didn't know that until after I met you. I promise you that." He raised my chin until I was looking him in the eye. "I promise," he repeated. I looked away and nodded reluctantly.

"But it wouldn't have changed anything if I had," he resumed. "I'm not going to make Cal's decisions for him. If he wants to do this, then we'll see if he's cut out for it. Maybe he won't be, like you say. But if he is," he said gently, "then it's his choice."

I looked away from his penetrating gaze. I couldn't speak. I hated what was happening. I hated it so much. But in spite of myself, a part of me had to admit that Grey was right. Tears sprang to my eyes again, and I swallowed and fought to keep them back. Then, with a gentleness that surprised me, Grey's thumb brushed against my cheek. His head bent, and his lips came down on mine.

Before I knew what I was doing, I was returning his kiss. His tongue find mine, his beard rough against my skin. I moaned into his mouth as he reached back and fisted my fingers in his hair. It was as though we were devouring each other. I lost myself in him, and when he broke the kiss I was left breathless, panting.

He groaned my name: "Seton. Christ, Seton."

I told myself to stop. I told myself to remember why I was there. But when his lips moved to my neck, everything else just fell away.

His breath singed my skin as he began to kiss and lick at my neck and the soft, vulnerable lobe of my ear. I shuddered as I felt his lips travel further down toward the hollow of my collar bone, tasting me as he went. It felt like my insides had turned to liquid, and the throbbing between my legs was so intense that I wondered in a haze if I would come just like this. I heard myself moaning, but I wasn't in control of any of the sounds that escaped me.

Grey's other hand moved up to my breast, cupping it. He growled in appreciation. "Fuck, Seton, you're so goddamn gorgeous. Do you have any idea how much I've thought about this?"

My only reply was a moan as his mouth moved lower, skimming my nipple through my T-shirt and bra. It felt like fire. I threw back my head and moaned his name. "Greyson, God, please…"

His teeth nipped through the fabric at my nipple, which felt as hard as a diamond under his touch. Each little nip sent an electric current through my body that ran straight to my core. The throbbing between my legs grew even more intense, and for a moment, I was sure I was going to come like that if he continued. But I needed more. So much more. "Greyson," I whimpered urgently.

He seemed to know exactly what I wanted. Leaning me back against the desk, he swept an arm behind me and cleared everything off the top of it. Objects fell to the floor with a crash. I should have been worried that the noise would bring someone, but I didn't care. I was too far gone. He reached up and pulled my T-shirt off over my head, and with a flick of his fingers the bra was unhooked, and soon that was gone, too, and I was lying there in front of him, naked from the waist up. Greyson drew back for a second to look at me. "God damn, woman," he said in a low growl. "You are going to be the death of me."

He lay me back on the table and moved over me. "I've been waiting for this," he mutters. His eyes were hooded with desire, his half-grin animal, almost savage. My lips parted involuntarily, and then his head came down and he began to tease my nipples, first one and then the other. His lips lightly nibbled me, his tongue flicking at the sensitive nubs, and I cried out. My hands went to his hair and I held him there. The pleasure was almost unbearable. I wanted it never to stop, but I wanted… I *needed*… so much more. My moans became increasingly desperate, the throb between my legs becoming an ache that begged to be relieved.

"Please…" I whispered again.

"Tell me what you want," he growled, his lips brushing against my nipples as he spoke. "Tell me. I want to hear it."

"Greyson, please," I said urgently. "Please make me come. I can't take anymore."

He raised his head and moved up until we were face to face. Instinctively, I spread my legs, thrusting my hips upward to meet his hardness. It felt so good that I gasped, and thrust again, desperate for relief. He was huge with need, hard as steel, and his dark eyes told me beyond a shadow of a doubt how much he wanted me.

"Remember what I told you last time?" he growled.

"Yes," I said breathlessly. If only he knew how many times I'd brought myself to orgasm thinking about it.

"I told you I was going to lick your pussy until you came, and then I was going to fuck you like you've never been fucked before."

"Yes," I said again. I needed it so badly.

He laughed, a low throaty sound. "Buckle up, sweetheart."

He unbuttoned my shorts, pulling them roughly over my hips, then stepped back to look at me. "Blue," he said, a slight grin playing across his face.

"What?" I asked, confused.

"Nothing," he said, chuckling. Then, in one motion, he reached down with both hands and ripped the fabric of my panties, tearing them off of me. My eyes widened as he growled in satisfaction. He traced one finger slowly up my thigh, the softest touch possible, and I gasped and writhed at his touch. My legs widened involuntarily as his finger found my center. "Jesus…" he hissed. "You're so fucking wet. You're so wet for me."

I almost felt embarrassed, but then his finger began to trace a pattern from my opening up to my desperate clit, and I cried out in pleasure, lifting my hips toward his touch. He grabbed my thighs and pushed me back on the desk until my legs were spread and my feet were on the surface. He stopped and looked at me, and his tongue licked across his lips in anticipation. I started to close my legs, momentarily self-conscious, but he barked, "Stop. Don't move."

I froze like that as I watched him undo the top button of his jeans, then the next, until the soft, worn fabric fell away to the floor. Underneath, he was not wearing underwear, and his erection snapped to attention before me. My eyes widened at the full glory of him: the muscular, tattooed chest, the hard, taut abs, his gorgeous, thick cock. I wanted so much, I wanted everything, right now. I reached for him but he shook his head. "No. Not yet."

Then he spread my legs and leaned down, and I lost what little control I still possessed. His tongue began to lick a path up my inner thigh, slowing as it reached my clit. He teased me, drawing circles around it but avoiding the spot that he knew I wanted him to touch, and I whimpered and tried to move toward him. With an impatient sound, he grabbed my hips and braced me so I can't move, then continued his torture, tongue flicking and teasing until I was afraid I'd lose my mind.

Then, when I was about to cry out in frustration, his tongue moved to the spot I so needed it to find. I gasped as he began to tease my clit, lapping at it, sucking it into his mouth, loving it. I moaned and thrashed, needing to come so desperately but at the same time wanting it to go on forever. He pulled away for a moment, sensing I was on the edge, then after a second resumed teasing me. I was panting, my breasts rising and falling rapidly as I hurtled closer and closer to the edge. A low groan escaped him, vibrating against my skin, and I cried out again. I felt his hand leave my hip then, and from the motion of his arm I realized he had begun to stroke himself slowly as he licked and tasted me. The image of his hand stroking his rock hard cock was too much for me to bear, and I shattered, calling out his name as I came in wave after wave.

I was still coming when Grey stood and reached into the desk drawer. I was dimly aware of the rustle of a condom wrapper, and then he was inside me, filling me as I continue to come. Grey groaned sharply as he entered me, and my hips raised to meet his as he began to thrust, hard, violent thrusts that made me come harder. He groaned my name and thrust a final time, and then I felt him pulse inside me as he came. I clung to his arms as they held my hips. It felt like the world had stopped spinning.

I have no idea how long we remained like that, breathing heavily, waiting for our hearts to stop pounding. Eventually, Grey reached down and gathered me up in his arms. His lips found mine and he kissed me, deeply, almost tenderly. I returned his kiss, wondering even as I did what in God's name I had just gotten myself into.

CHAPTER 10

Grey

I didn't want her to go.

That was a first.

Women don't get to me. Not like this. I'm usually thinking about something else by the time I zip up my pants. I don't have time for hearts and flowers. I've got a club to run. Business is business. Pussy is pussy. I can't mix the two. It's too dangerous.

But Seton Greenlee had gotten under my skin. She was like an itch I couldn't scratch: she was always there in my head, even when I was doing my damnedest to get her the hell out of there.

When we both eventually caught our breath after I took her hard in my office, there was a lull in conversation that, in hindsight, I should have expected. How do you go from having sex so fucking fantastic you think your head might explode off your neck, to making chit-chat? Especially when there was a subject of conversation so fraught with tension that neither of you wanted to return to it? I was no good at social niceties anyway, never had been. So, in silence, I pulled my pants up from around my ankles and watched Seton as she looked around for her clothes. I reached down and grabbed her T-shirt, her bra, and her shorts, and handed them all to her. She rewarded me with a shy duck of her head. I nodded toward the pathetic shred of fabric that still lay on the floor. "Sorry about your panties," I muttered.

To my surprise, instead of blushing, Seton smiled. "That's okay," she said softly, her eyes twinkling mischievously. "I wasn't all that attached to them. And," she continued with a wicked little grin that surprised me, "I think the trade-off was worth it."

Our eyes locked, and the moment of merriment dissolved in a burst of heat. Damned if I didn't want to take her all over again, from every position I could think of, until both of us passed out from exhaustion. But she pulled her eyes away from mine and stood up, pulling her T-shirt over her head. "Maybe I should just put this on," she said, her voice husky with suppressed desire.

We continued dressing in silence. My mind was swirling around in all different directions, trying to make sense of everything. What it all meant. So, I did what I usually did when things got complicated. I pushed it all aside. I concentrated on this moment alone.

"Seton," I murmured, drawing her to me.

She looked up at me, her sparkling eyes almost luminescent. "Grey," she responded.

Somehow, it seemed as though we had an entire conversation with just those two words. I kissed her again, deeply. Her arms wound around my neck almost instinctively, her body melted into mine like we were made from the same mold. I hardened against her. She whimpered and pressed against me. The heat grew between us.

After a few moments, she pulled away, breathing heavily. "I should go," she whispered.

I didn't ask why, or try to make her stay. I knew this was all confusing as hell for her. Hell, it was no picnic for me, either.

"Okay," I said. I let her detach herself from me, and watched in silence as she walked slowly toward the door and opened it. She stood in the threshold for a moment and looked back at me. My heart felt like it was going to beat out of my chest, but I said nothing. She nodded once at me, and I nodded back. Then she was gone.

Holy hell. I sank into my chair. Lacing my fingers behind my head, I blew out a deep breath and kicked my feet up on the desk. This shit was complicated. Maybe even dangerous.

I was falling for Seton Greenlee.

I couldn't see this ending well. If I'd had a brain in my head, I'd just end it right now. Hell, I wasn't even sure if there was an "it" to end. But I had just crossed a line, and even though fucking a woman had never felt like it was an act with consequences before, fucking *this* woman was different. I might have been able to deny that before, but now, I couldn't hide it from myself any longer. I never would have thought in a million goddamn years that a woman would be able to turn me inside out with just a look.

And then I finally meet the one who can, and she's the absolute last person who should be involved with a piece of shit like me.

I was going to be sending her brother out on dangerous runs. As the club president, I was potentially going to be putting his life in danger. And every time I did it, I would potentially be breaking Seton's heart.

Then there was the fact of the secrets between us. Secrets she didn't even know existed.

I had tried to come clean with her. I told her I knew about her dad, and about his death and the connection to the club. But I didn't come even anywhere near close to telling her the truth.

Seton was proud. You could see that in her eyes. Her fucking gorgeous, whip-smart, defiant eyes. She didn't want help from anyone. And she sure as hell didn't want anyone knowing her secrets.

Trouble was, I knew them already. And I had a few of my own.

I knew she hated that Cal was prospecting with the Stone Kings. I knew that she barely tolerated that I was one of them. Let alone the president of the damn club.

What would she do if she knew it was not just a member of the club who killed her father, but my uncle? What would she say, how would she react, if she knew that I was there that day? That I saw her at her most vulnerable moment, in what was probably the sharpest agony of her life?

I shook my head and swore. There was no way this was going to turn out good between Seton and me.

The eyes of that little girl crying over her dad's body had haunted me for years. I knew that Clayton Greene's death wouldn't have affected me much if not for the memory of her eyes. Everyone in town knew Greene was a worthless piece of shit. He drank from morning till night, got in bar fights regularly, and couldn't hold a job for longer than a few months. He was charming when sober and sloppy as hell when drunk. If not for Seton, I might have thought his death was just as well. But even though I didn't know her, watching her sob over her father's body — the shock of suddenly seeing Clayton Greene as a father, with people who had loved him — it stuck with me. Even now, when I sent my guys out on a run, I thought about them as family men, as sons and fathers, brothers and cousins, as well as club members. And even though I didn't let it affect my decisions — I couldn't — it helped me not make those decisions lightly. It helped me to take the full measure of the men I sent out into harm's way in the name of the Stone Kings MC.

I started to feel restless, so I left my office and called to a couple of the brothers that I was going out on a ride. I hopped on the bike and turned it toward the west side of town, out past the city limits in the direction of the mountains. As I rode, I thought about Cal. I wasn't sure how to feel about him. His good looks and his charmer personality reminded me of his father, though he didn't seem to have the same weakness for the drink. I even liked the kid; he made me laugh with his combination of earnestness and swaggering self-confidence.

After what had happened with Jethro, I had to be doubly damn sure about anyone new we took into the club. I knew it was a risk that I'd be softer on him because of how I felt about Seton. I couldn't afford that, and neither could the club. I'd have to police myself, make sure he proved himself beyond a shadow of a doubt as a prospect, or he'd have to go. The ride out into Cannibals territory would be a good first step.

When I got to the club, I went to find Trig, who told me that the ride was planned for two days from now. "Frankenstein and Cal are both up for it. They know what the plan is, why we're doing it, and they're ready."

"Good," I approved. "Give them both guns for the trip."

"Guns?" Trig repeated. "Sure, prez, but shit, they're still doin' beer runs and washin' our bikes. You sure you want to ramp 'em up this fast?"

"I'm not ramping 'em up," I retorted. I took out a smoke and lit it. "I want you to see how they do with this. If they get cocky, don't take the shit seriously, I want you to tell me about it. You know guns make men stupid as shit. I want to see what they're like when we let them play in the big sand box."

"Sure thing, prez," he said. I wasn't sure if Trig completely agreed with me, but he didn't argue. Trig was a VP I could count on. He was with me all the way, would carry out my orders without question. He had never openly challenged a decision I had made, but I still relied on his counsel, and I knew that when he offered a different opinion, it was damn worth considering.

I nodded once to confirm the plan, then continued as I lit a smoke. "Make sure Repo knows they're to be packing, too. Just in case something goes down, make sure you've talked through a game plan with the prospects. Make sure they know exactly what their role is, exactly what they can and cannot do. They deviate from that plan by one fucking hair, you let me know."

Trig nodded. "Got it." He gave me a speculative look, and then drew a breath. "You know," he began quietly, "no one blames you for Jethro."

"*I* blame me for Jethro," I growled. I did not want to talk about this shit now. "I should have never sponsored that fucker in the first place."

"He came highly recommended," Trig murmured. "You trusted your uncle."

"Yeah, well that's where I went wrong." Jethro had come from my uncle Lawless's chapter in Reno, asking to be patched over to us because his ex-wife and kid lived close to Lupine. Even though I didn't have much of a relationship with Lawless, I let his recommendation sway me. *If we hadn't let Jethro into the club, Hammer would still be alive today,* I reminded myself for the hundredth time. Family relationship or not, I had fucked up taking any man's word for something so important. I should have tested Jethro more. He should have had to prove to me and the club that he wasn't a goddamn coward. He should have proven he would risk his life for the club, before the club risked their lives for him.

Those days were over, I told myself, taking another angry drag of my smoke. I was through letting emotions into my decisions. No matter how I felt about Seton Greenlee, no matter how much I knew she worried about him, Cal would have to earn his spot in the Stone Kings. The hard way.

CHAPTER 11

Seton

For the third time in three days, I was crying.

I didn't cry. Ever. Not since the weeks after my father had died. Only at sad movies, but that didn't count. I never cried for myself. Not even when things got really shitty. I had a handle on my emotions. I had learned through experience that letting your emotions get the better of you would hurt you in the end.

Carly was at the apartment when I got home, so I murmured a quick hello and made a beeline for my room before she could notice anything wrong and start questioning me. I'd been sitting on my bed quietly sobbing ever since.

After my attempt to get Grey to push Cal out of the club ended in us having mind-bending sex on his desk, I had left the clubhouse reeling with emotions. Greyson Stone was the absolute last man in the world I should be getting involved with. Every time I was around him, I seemed to lose my damn mind, and things would go pretty much exactly the opposite of how I wanted them to.

Not that I hadn't wanted what had happened, I had to admit to myself. And that was the whole problem. My body flushed with heat at the memory of what he had done to me. How I had called out his name as he licked me to orgasm. How he had found his release inside me with a roar as we clung to one another. I had never felt anything even remotely like I felt when Grey Stone touched me. And now that I knew what it was like with him, I had no idea how I'd find the strength to stay away from him.

I pulled another Kleenex from the box and blew my nose. Why was the one person who had ever made me feel like a woman — a real, sexy, desirable woman — the one person in all of Lupine I should stay furthest away from?

But that wasn't even the main reason I was crying. How did my life turn to such complete and utter shit so quickly?

Ever since the fight Cal and I had had the other night at dinner, I had done a lot of thinking about our family, and the ways us three kids had always been so different growing up. Reed, the oldest, had always been sullen and quiet as a kid. Cal, had always been a tow-headed charmer and a clown as a young boy. As a baby, we couldn't take a trip to the grocery store without strangers cooing and making goofy faces at him in the checkout line. As a boy, he would get away with murder with the neighbors no matter what his childish crime. All he had to do was flash a dazzling, gap-toothed smile, and pretty soon the neighbor lady whose window he had broken was sitting him down at her kitchen table for milk and cookies. As he got older, he grew from an unusually cute child to a strikingly handsome adolescent. In teen years he would eventually realize that girls would drop their panties for him at the drop of a crooked smile. The fact that he seemed to always be in some sort of trouble, for vandalizing, or smoking weed, seemed to only make him more attractive to the teen girls who fantasized about taming the sexy bad boy.

Even my mom was more indulgent with Cal than she ever was with Reed and me. To be honest, Cal was the only one of the three of us that she seemed to care for very much. She even seemed to take his run-ins with the law relatively in stride, neglecting to punish him until eventually he wound up in juvenile court and had to serve some time in a facility for minors. Even after he came out, my mother just let him run wild, saying Cal was just being a boy, and that he'd straighten out in time.

It would have been easy to resent Cal for that, but he wore others' adoration of him so lightly that it was hard to begrudge him anything. But I'd be lying if I said that watching my Mom's relative softheartedness toward Cal didn't make my miss my dad and his the memory of his love for me even more.

When I was young, I didn't even know my dad was an alcoholic, really. I just knew that he smelled funny sometimes and liked to drink things that tasted bitter. I just knew that he loved me and called me his Little Girl, and that he always had a special smile just for me when he came home.

Sometimes, when he was in a good mood and just wanted to stop into a bar for a drink or two, he would bring me with him, and give me money to play video games while he laughed and chatted with the other men in the bar. He would introduce me to the men, and they would call me by my name and my dad would tell them how smart I was, and I'd feel proud. I was too young to know there was anything strange about him bringing a child with him to a bar so he could drink. I only knew it was one of the only times I felt noticed and special.

I used to blame my mother for my dad's death, at first. A child's thinking is mostly black and white, after all, and my dad had to be blameless in my young, lonely eyes, because he was gone and because I needed him to remain my hero. So my quiet resentment of my mother stewed in my young mind, and the distance grew between us little by little. Maggie didn't really seem to notice, or at least didn't make much of an effort to bridge the gap between us, until by the time I was grown she felt more like a guardian to me than a mother. So when she moved to Scottsdale with Cal after I graduated from high school, leaving me to fend for myself at college, I was only a little bit hurt, and not really surprised.

My argument with Cal the other day hadn't been far from my thoughts since it happened, and I had been ruminating about how much his words about my father had hurt me. At first, I was so angry I could barely contemplate ever being able to talk to Cal again. But as I worked to get my emotions under control, I had begun to think about our family, and how different all of our experiences must have been of my father's death. Since my mom had refused to talk about Dad after he died, us kids were left to do our own individual mourning in solitude. Reed and I had never been close, so we had never confided our feelings to each other about anything, much less our father's death. And Cal had been so young when Dad was killed, I'm not even sure he really understood what had happened. One day Daddy was there, and the next he was gone. I realized now that Cal must have had very few memories of him, if any.

I realized, too, that Cal had a very different and in many ways better relationship to Mom than Reed and I did, even as adults. After all, she had taken Cal with her when she moved to Scottsdale. He had lived with her there for all of his high school years. Cal had had a whole chapter of his life with her in Arizona that didn't include me at all. In a way, it was understandable that he didn't see Dad's death in quite the same way I did. And as much as I hated to do it, I had to admit to myself that the truth about what had happened was probably somewhere in the middle. I tried to picture what it must have been like for Maggie Greenlee, being married to an unreliable alcoholic and saddled with three kids that she must have felt she was raising all by herself. The more I tried to imagine how hard her life must have been, I came to the point where I no longer blamed her, exactly, for what had happened. The damage between her and me was done, but I could at least recognize that she was only human. And that Calvin's memory and my memory of our childhoods would always be different.

All of these thoughts had left me feeling raw, and in some ways even more barren and bereft than before. The history of my family that I had understood, the story that I had always told myself, was only one interpretation — mine, and mine alone. It made me feel like the ground I stood on was even shakier than before. But it was all the ground I had to stand on, and I had to accept that.

The day after I had gone to see Grey at the clubhouse — this morning, to be exact — I decided to pay Cal a visit and try to make amends. I didn't know what I was going to say when I got there, exactly, but I didn't like the way we had left things. As angry as I was at him for calling our father a drunk, I regretted kicking him out of my apartment. Cal was basically my only family, given that my mother didn't seem to care one way or another about me, and Reed was AWOL. And I didn't want to erase any of the shaky foundation that he was trying to rebuild between us.

Cal was out in the driveway of the house he shared with a couple of other guys, working on his motorcycle, when I pulled up to the curb. He seemed guarded as he watched me get out of the car and stride up the walk toward him. "Hey, sis," he murmured, his expression neutral

"Hi," I replied. I worked to keep my voice light and friendly. "Whatcha doing?" I asked, nodding toward his bike.

"Just got done checking the air filter." He eyed me curiously and grabbed a rag that was sitting on the seat of his bike to wipe his hands. "Nothing major."

"I see," I said. I glanced at the bike. "It's looking good."

"Thanks." He stuffed the rag in his pocket and looked at me. "So. What's up?"

I sighed and sat down on the front stoop. "I wanted to apologize for the other night, Cal. I was out of line."

Cal raised one eyebrow. "That's a surprise."

I looked down, embarrassed. "I know. I'm sure you thought I was expecting one from you."

He chuckled. "Yeah, pretty much. Honestly, See, I shouldn't have said what I did about Dad. I know you were close to him."

I looked at him in disbelief.

"Yeah. I do," he continued. "I was pretty young when he died, so I don't remember much about him. But I remember how sad you were. I remember how much you changed. How serious you got. I know it's because you missed him."

My eyes filled with tears, and I brushed at them with the back of my hand. "Yeah. I... I still miss him so much, Cal." I took a deep breath and let it out. "But I don't want this…" I motioned to the bike, "to come between us. You're basically the only family I have left."

He sat down beside me on the stoop. "There's Mom. And Reed… sort of," he trailed off.

"You know as well as I do Mom doesn't really care about me. And we may never see Reed again."

Cal opened his mouth to protest, then shut it. "Mom does care about you," he finally managed. "She just… doesn't know how to express it."

I scoffed. "Well, when she figures it out, I'll be right here, waiting."

Cal looked down at his hands. "I'm sorry, See. I know you and mom… well." He broke off, embarrassed. "And I know I haven't been a very good brother."

"That's not what I meant," I reassured him. "It's just… I'm worried about you. And I guess I don't know how not to be. The club… it scares me. And not just because of what happened to Dad."

"What happened to Dad wasn't because of the club," Cal retorted. He glanced at me, a look of apology in his eyes, then continued more gently. "It wasn't the club that killed him, See. It was a man. He's not even in the club anymore. I heard he's somewhere in Nevada. Reno, I think." He turned to me then, his expression firm, his square jaw set. "Look, Seton, I know you think I'm still five years old, but I'm an adult. I'm a man. It's time for me to make my own choices. I know you don't like some of them, but you'll just have to live with that."

He stood then, and without waiting for my response grabbed the leather cut that was lying beside him on the stoop. Putting it on, he turned to me. "I have to go," he said. His tone was calm, but firm. "Thank you for coming over, See. Really." He looked me in the eye. "I mean it. I'll talk to you soon, okay?"

"Okay," I whispered. He straddled the bike and fired it up. He pulled the used rag out of his back pocket and threw it on the lawn beside him, and as he did, I caught a glimpse of the gun stuck in the waistband of his jeans.

I watched him drive away to whatever awaited him, wondering whether the club that had taken away my father was about to take my brother as well.

CHAPTER 12

Grey

Trig and Repo took the prospects on a ride north into Cannibals territory the next day. They had armed them both with a couple of Walther P99s and spent the afternoon before making sure that both Frankenstein and Cal knew at least the basics of how to use them. Trig told me that Frankenstein could barely hit the side of a barn with a handgun, but he was much better with a shotgun. Cal, he said, had obviously shot before and showed some promise with the Walther.

I spent that day trying to keep my thoughts on the club and off of Seton. I knew that I had to keep her and her brother totally separate in my mind, but frankly, I was doing a piss poor job of it. But what was worse, it damn near killed me to think about what I was pretty sure was inevitable: that sooner or later, she would find out about my family's role in her father's death. Once she figured it out, or once I told her myself, I was sure that would be it between us. Hell, if I had any balls at all, I would just come right out with it and tell her. Rip the Band-aid off and be done with it. After all, I told myself, this thing between us wasn't anything permanent. We both knew it couldn't last. Better to just accept it and move on.

But every time I started to think about doing just that, the memory of how good it had felt being inside her stopped me in my tracks.

My dick pressed hard and insistent at my zipper at the memory of her moaning underneath me. I shifted uncomfortably on the seat of my bike in response and goosed the engine as I coasted down the highway. I hadn't seen her since I had spread her legs in my back office and made her scream my name, then pressed myself inside that sweet hot center of her and come so hard I thought I'd lose consciousness. It was killing me to not just turn my bike around and head back into Lupine to find her, but I needed to have the run into Cannibal territory over and done with before I could let myself think about Seton. I knew, though, that the second the run was finished and the boys were on their way back to Lupine, I'd be on my way to see her.

I forced my thoughts away from Seton once again, and back to the MC. Trigger and Repo had been gone about three hours, and I hadn't heard word from Trig yet. That in itself wasn't anything to be concerned about.

I expected them to be gone for at least six or seven hours, and if all went well, I might not hear from them until this evening, anyway.

But I was antsy, more so than usual, and as much as I hated to admit it to myself, I attributed my edginess to Seton's brother being on the run. Part of me wished I hadn't sent the prospects on with Trig and Repo. But the other part of me — the MC president — knew that I wouldn't have hesitated to send a prospect into danger to test their mettle. Then again, I wondered, was I fooling myself? Had I sent the prospects out on that run on purpose, to prove to myself that the memory of Seton Greenlee's pouty, fuckable mouth and the way she looked deep into my eyes as I came inside her hadn't clouded my brain? I thought back to Trigger's surprise at my decision to send the prospects. Would it have been smarter to send him and Repo by themselves, without two untested and inexperienced men with them?

I swore under my breath. This was no good. I couldn't let myself start second-guessing my decisions. What was done was done. I had sent the four of them on the run; now what would happen, would happen. I throttled up and took the next corner a little faster than normal, just to shake my head free of all my thoughts, and concentrated on thinking about nothing but the road ahead.

About an hour later, my phone began to buzz. I got off the highway and came to stop at the edge of a bank of pines. I looked at the screen: Trigger.

"Yeah," I barked into it.

"Hey, prez. Wanted to give you an update," Trigger responded. "Just exited Cannibal territory. We took ourselves a nice, slow Sunday drive to Crow Wing."

"Any trouble?" I asked.

"None," came the answer. Relief coursed through me. "We even drove past the bar they hang out at over on the east side of town. A bunch of bikes were in the parking lot, even some Cannibals hanging out in front having a smoke. They watched us drive by. No confrontation. Not even a warning escort out of town."

I frowned. "That's good," I said. "Maybe too good."

"Yeah," he agreed. "My thought, too. They just watched us drive by. Seemed a little strange they didn't at least stop us for a little chat. We even drove nice and slow so they had plenty of time to catch up with us. Nothing."

"Huh." I wasn't sure what to make of that. Of all the possible reactions from the Cannibals I had expected, this wasn't one of them. "Okay," I continued. "Come on back, then. I want to see you, Levi, Winger, Moose and Repo tomorrow. We need to discuss next steps."

"You got it, prez," Trigger replied.

I ended the call and sat back on the bike to think. I tried to keep my mind off of Seton even as I breathed a sigh of relief that her brother hadn't been harmed, and focus on the problem at hand. Drawing a deep breath, I let it out slowly and deliberately. Okay. Maybe the Cannibals had had nothing to do with Hammer's death. If they had, it would have stood to reason that the attack would have been the opening salvo in a war. In which case, they wouldn't have let Trigger and the others ride through their town without a response. Then again, even if the Cannibals weren't behind the attack, it was unusual to say the least that they hadn't reacted to our presence in their territory. Their lack of reaction in itself could be considered a reaction of another kind. In which case, the response might still be to come.

Also, even it was good news that the brothers hadn't run into any danger, that left us back at square one in terms of figuring out who had been behind the shootout. As I sat there trying to puzzle my way through the Cannibals' lack of response another, my thoughts went to Jethro. The night of the attack, he had fled at the first sounds of gun shot. At least, that's what he had told Trigger and Levi when they tracked him down as he was packing his bags to skip town. And what he told me later, when they brought him in hands bound behind his back and face bloodied and beaten, to see me.

At the time, I had been so furious at his betrayal of my best friend and the MC that meting out club justice had been the only thing on my mind. But now, as I sat looking out at the tall pine forest, I wondered if Jethro had known more than he said he did? Was it possible that he had known who was behind the attack? For the first time, I wondered whether his "escape" had been something else entirely. He had paid the ultimate price for abandoning a brother, but had he gotten away with another kind of betrayal?

Fuck. I couldn't believe the thought had never occurred to me. The possibility that Jethro might have been not just a coward, but a mole as well, made my blood boil in my veins. I felt like punching something. Jethro was lucky he was dead, I thought to myself grimly. If he was still alive, he would probably be begging for me to end him before I was through with him.

It was too late to find out now, of course; I would probably never know if Jethro had been working for someone else. But if it was even a possibility, that made the entire landscape look different. I didn't like the feeling of being in the dark, like there were shadows everywhere. Problem with shadows was, you were tempted to shoot at them, but you could get shot yourself if you got distracted and aimed in the wrong direction.

I started the bike back up and gunned it, then pulled back out on the highway in the direction of Lupine. Tomorrow I'd talk to the officers and get more information from Trigger. I knew there was no making a decision now.

As I approached the city limits of Lupine, though, instead of turning my bike toward the clubhouse, I went in the other direction. Toward the Cactus Bar. Seton had mentioned she was working tonight. I wanted to see her. I knew how much it bothered her that her brother was a prospect with the MC, and somehow, even though I knew she didn't know anything about the run he had just gone on, I still felt the need to reassure her, somehow. My plan was just to go down there and have a beer. Just have a normal conversation about nothing, so she'd know everything was fine.

Just one beer. That was all. In and out.
Sure.

CHAPTER 13

Seton

I had been at work barely two hours, and already I had broken one wine glass and dropped a mug full of beer on the floor. I just couldn't seem to keep my hands from shaking as I thought about where Cal might be right now. I had texted him an hour ago, but still hadn't received a response. He had been much better about getting back to me the last week or so, and I couldn't help but think that he was going silent on me now to protect me from things he thought I wouldn't want to know.

My case of nerves hadn't gone unnoticed by my boss. "Seton, get your shit together," Wes barked at me.

"You want me to start taking what you break out of your paycheck?"

Normally, I would have ignored Wes's petty comments, but today I wasn't having it. "Shut up, Wes," I retorted.

"Watch yourself," he warned.

"Or what?" I snapped. I just didn't have the patience to tiptoe around Wes right now. I threw down my rag and glared at him. "You'll fire me? Go ahead, Wes. I'm not in the mood to be treated like a child. You think I'm breaking stuff on purpose?" I grabbed a martini glass from the counter and held it in the air, threatening with my eyes to send it crashing to the ground. "Do you really think that?"

Wes whistled in mock surprise. "Jesus, okay, calm down," he said, raising his hands. "Though," he continued, his expression morphing from a scowl to a leer, "You're pretty sexy when you're angry."

"Fuck off, Wes," Andi snarled beside me.

"You, too, sugarplum," he shot back. He threw a mocking wink in her direction, then, turned back down the hall toward his office.

"Christ almighty, what a perv," Andi muttered at his retreating back. She looked back toward me then, her eyes registering her concern. "You okay, See? You seem super on edge today."

I looked at her, taking in the worried expression on her face. It was on the tip of my tongue to tell her I was fine and change the subject, but something stopped me.

The fact was, I was exhausted from trying to pretend like nothing was wrong.

"I am on edge," I admitted. "I'm… ugh, Andi, I'm just… there's just a ton going on right now."

"You want to talk about it?" she asked.

I hesitated. Andi glanced out at the room. About half of the tables were full, and the waitresses were busy serving drinks and meals from the kitchen. "Okay, spill," she said, leaning against the bar.

"It's a long story," I protested.

"No worries," she smiled.

I told her the bare bones version of my visit to Cal's house, including how I'd seen the handgun he'd shoved into the waistband of his jeans. Andi looked at me in alarm. "Whoa. What did he say about the gun?"

"I didn't ask him about it," I said miserably. "I didn't really have time. He jumped on his bike and rode away. And honestly, what would I have even said about it? He knows I'm not comfortable with him prospecting with the club. He would have just gotten defensive. It's not like his big sister disapproving would have changed anything."

"Probably not," Andi conceded. "Shit, See, I'm sorry."

"And… that's not all," I said, then stopped, suddenly regretting saying even that much. But Andi knew me well, and she could be a bulldog when she wanted to. I knew she wasn't going to let me stop talking once I'd started.

"What? Seton, come on. Tell me what's up," she ordered.

I sighed again. "There's... there's a guy..."

Andi whooped, the sound attracting the attention of half the bar. "Sorry!" she called merrily, then turned back to me. "Tell me! Oh, my God, tell me you've found someone better than Asshole Nate!"

"I'm... I'm not sure if I've 'found' anybody. And as for being better than Nate... well, he's certainly different," I said wryly.

"Who is he?" she prompted. "Where did you meet him?"

I stared at her and forced myself to open my mouth. "He's the president of the Stone Kings."

"WHAT?!" Andi yelled. The customers turned around again to look at her. "Oh, mind your own business!" she snapped at them, rolling her eyes. She looked back at me, her voice lower now but no less animated. "Jesus, Seton, are you serious? You are with the president of the MC?"

"I'm not 'with' anybody," I corrected. "Not exactly, anyway. Oh, Andi, I don't know what's going on!" I wailed. "He... I met him when Cal borrowed my car and didn't return it. He left it at the MC's clubhouse and I went to pick it up, and Grey was there..."

"Grey Stone?" she said, her eyes widening.

"Do you know him?" I asked quizzically.

"Yeah, I've seen him around. I knew he was in the MC, but I guess I didn't know he was the president." Her eyes widened. "He's hot! Holy hell, Seton!" She leaned in, her tone turning conspiratorial. "Have you… you know?"

At my lack of response, she threw her head back and laughed out loud. "Oh, my God, you've been banging a biker!" she cried.

"Shhhh!" I warned, looking around me in alarm. "Stop it, Andi, I'm serious!"

"I'm sorry, I'm sorry!" she said. Her eyes continued to twinkle as she continued in a lower voice. "So, how was it?"

"Fantastic," I admitted shyly.

"Oh my God!" she laughed. "So, what's the problem again?"

"Andi! My brother's in the MC. I can't… I can't be *doing* this with the president of the club when I'm trying to get Cal out of it!"

"Oh, yeah. Oh, sorry, I kind of lost the plot in my excitement about the sexy biker guy. You do know you're kind of living a fantasy of mine, right?" she grinned.

"Andi, come on! Be serious!"

"Oh, girl, I *am* serious." She took a deep breath and let it out. "But, I see your point. So, what are you going to do?"

"I don't know. That's just the problem."

"Do you want to keep seeing Grey Stone?"

"I don't know that either," I said miserably. "I mean, there's like this… electricity when I'm around him. It's unlike anything I've ever felt. But at the same time, God, every relationship I've been in has been with someone irresponsible and unreliable. And now I start something with the president of a biker gang? Like, what's next, an ex-con?"

"Hey, don't judge," Andi admonished. "Maybe deep down he's a family man who dreams of a white picket fence and two point five kids."

I scrunched up my nose. "I don't think so. It's hard to imagine Grey mowing the lawn."

She giggled. "True. So, what are you going to do?"

Shaking my head, I shrugged my shoulders in frustration. "Beats me."

"Well, then," Andi said, ever practical, "Try not to think about it for now. Just go with the flow. Eventually, a path will open up. You'll know what to do when it does."

I cocked an eyebrow at her. "Since when are you so philosophical?"

"I have depths of intelligence you have never experienced," she said modestly. "Seriously, though. Just let it go for now. You don't have to decide everything right this instant. Take a deep breath, and tell yourself what will be will be."

"Thank you, Doris Day," I mocked. But despite the fact that I was no closer to making any decisions, I felt better for having talked to my best friend. I went about the rest of my shift feeling a little lighter, and determined to try hard not to think about things I couldn't do anything about.

I had hoped to avoid Wes after my angry outburst, but just my luck, he came out to the bar a little over an hour later and leaned over the counter. "Seton, I need to see you in the back. Andi, you're on your own for a few minutes."

"Whatever you say, Boss." Andi gave him a mocking two-fingered salute, but he had already turned away. She shot me a quizzical look and I shrugged and followed Wes back to the office. I wondered if I had pushed him far enough that he was planning to fire me. The thought should have worried me, but at that point I had enough other things on my mind that the possibility didn't really faze me much.

Instead of sitting behind his ratty old metal desk like he usually did, Wes shut the door and leaned against the front of it, facing me. He crossed his arms, and in a voice that he obviously meant to be friendly, asked, "Seton, is there anything you'd like to tell me to explain your job performance today?"

The words should have pissed me off, but since he seemed like he was making an effort to be nice, I decided I'd try to return the sentiment. "No. I've got some stuff going on right now that's making me a little on edge, but I'll be okay. I'm sorry I let it affect my work," I said in what I hoped was a sincere tone. "I promise I'll do better."

Wes stood and moved closer, until he was standing barely a foot away from me. I took a subtle step back, hoping he wouldn't notice. "Hey, hey, Seton, no need to back away from me. I don't bite," he smiled, showing his teeth in a rat-like grin.

"I, uh, guess I'm just a little sensitive to my personal space," I stammered as he took another step toward me. He had pushed me against the chair in front of his desk, and the backs of my knees brushed against it. If I tried to move backwards any further, I would fall into it.

"You seem a little tense," he continued. His voice had taken on a slightly unctuous tone. "You sure you don't need a little tension release?" He reached up and awkwardly began to massage my shoulders. A shudder ran through me at his touch, and instinctively I reached up with both arms and shoved his hands away from me. "No, I don't need tension release. Please stop touching me," I said, as calmly as I could manage.

"Come on, Seton," he said then, his voice changing from wheedling to hard and demanding. "You know you want it." One arm went around me then, too quickly for me to react, and then he was pressing against me, his hardness pulsing against my leg.

I opened my mouth to scream, but his other hand clamped over my mouth before I could make much noise. I began to struggle frantically, my mind fighting to grasp that my boss was going to sexually assault me if I didn't get away somehow. "You don't want to lose your job, I know," he continued through gritted teeth as his grip tightened on me. "You can do something for me, and I'll do something for you."

Wes was stronger than he looked, and he was holding me so tightly against him now that I couldn't get my arms free. The short skirt I was wearing began to ride up from my struggling, and I shuddered as I realized that soon my panties would be exposed to his touch. I tried to maneuver my leg so that I could knee him in the crotch, but he pressed me against the back of the chair so I couldn't attempt it without losing balance.

I continued to struggle, but he held me fast. In desperation, I realized that my only hope was if I could destabilize both of us, so I said a silent prayer and then deliberately leaned back against the chair with enough force that Wes couldn't counteract the motion. I toppled backwards and he toppled after me, swearing and instinctively moving his hand away from my face to break his fall. I opened my mouth and screamed as loud as I could, my scream turning to a yelp of pain as I fell to the floor and cracked my head against the wooden planks.

Suddenly, the door flew open and a mountain of muscle flew at Wes, grabbing him by the shirt and hauling him to his feet. Grey Stone pulled back a fist and smashed it against Wes's face. I stumbled to my feet as Grey pulled back and took aim again, connecting with Wes's jaw with a sickening crack. Wes sank to the floor with a horrible gurgling sound coming from his throat. He weakly raised his hands as if to stop Grey from hitting him again, but Grey was on him in an instant. His face was frozen in a rictus of fury. Grabbing Wes by the collar once again and raising him up, he roared as he cocked his fist back a third time. Wes closed his eyes and screamed, bloody snot running down his lip.

"Grey, stop!" I said, beginning to sob. "Stop, you'll kill him!" I bent down and grabbed at his arm, struggling uselessly to subdue him. His muscle was cold, unmovable steel. Grey made a move to shake me off, but I clung harder. "Please, Grey!" I cried. "Don't!"

Eventually my plea seemed to sink in, and with a grunt of fury, Grey shook Wes's prone body one more time by the collar and threw him to the floor. Grey stood gazing at his bloodied face with a look of loathing. When he turned to me, unseeing, there was a dark, barely-contained rage in his eyes that frightened me. I resisted the urge to flinch. "Please," I whispered again. "Please stop now."

"What did he do to you?" Grey demanded, his voice as cold as ice.

"Nothing!" I insisted. "Not yet. He was going to…" my voice broke. "But he didn't do anything. I'm okay."

Wes turned back to the cowering figure on the floor. "You almost died today," he hissed. He leaned down toward Wes, who began to weep and shied away from the figure who towered over him. "You are done with women," Grey seethed, pointing a hard finger at him. "Completely. You understand that? You've just taken a permanent fucking vow of chastity."

Wes's eyes widened, and he nodded, his sobs growing louder.

Grey stood up, a profound look of disgust on his face. Wordlessly, he reached out and pulled me to him. I collapsed into his arms and realized I was shaking. Silently, he led me out of the office, Grey closing the door behind us with a final slam. We stopped in the hallway, and he reached up and began to stroke my hair. I forced myself to concentrate on breathing deeply and tried to compose myself. I inhaled, then exhaled, and his warmth and the clean, leathery scent of him began to calm me.

When I had stopped shaking, Grey pulled away and looked down at me. His eyes were still dark and angry, but there was something else there. Something I could tell was just for me. "Come on," he murmured gently. "We're leaving." He took my hand in his large, callused one, and led me down the hall. When we got out to the bar, he glanced at Andi, who was staring at us wide-eyed. "Your boss might need some medical attention," Grey grunted at her. Andi simply nodded and gave me a small wave as he led me out the door.

Out in the parking lot, he walked me to his motorcycle. "You okay to ride?" he asked. I nodded. Straddling the bike, he reached for the helmet hanging from the handlebar and handed it to me. "You know how to put this on?" he asked.

"I think so," I answered. I pulled the helmet over my head, and began to fumble with the straps. Grey gently pushed my hands away and snapped them together himself, adjusting them until they fit snugly under my chin. I looked at the bike seat, realizing that my skirt was so short that getting on it would be a challenge. Blushing, I yanked it down as much as I could and lifted up one leg, straddling the seat quickly.

I wrapped my arms around Grey's waist, closing my eyes for a moment as I breathed in the comforting scent of his leather cut. He started the engine, and I felt the rumble of it vibrate between my legs as he kicked the bike out of neutral and pulled out of the parking lot. I didn't know where we were going, and I didn't feel like asking. For just a little while, I only wanted to be there, with him, flying through the cool summer night.

CHAPTER 14

Grey

It was the closest I had ever come to killing a man with my bare hands.

If Seton's voice begging me to stop hadn't cut through the fog of rage that had surrounded me as I beat that little bag of shit senseless, I don't think I would have emerged from it. The sound of her terrified scream, the image of him on top of her were burned so clearly into my brain I didn't think I would ever forget them. I tried to suppress the rage that was still boiling in me, just under the surface, and throttled up, feeling the cool wind rush past my face. Behind me, Seton's grip tightened around my waist as she snuggled up closer against me.

Suddenly my mind flashed to what would have happened if I hadn't decided to go to the bar to see her. When I got to the Cactus, Seton's car was in the lot, so I knew she was working, but when I walked in she wasn't behind the bar. The other bartender, a tall girl with short blond hair and a good ass, told me she was in the back on break and motioned me through. I was standing in the hallway, figuring maybe she was in the ladies room, when I heard a thud and a muffled scream. When I slammed open the door and saw Seton on the floor with that fucking pig on top of her, I swear to God I would have shot him in a heartbeat if I'd had my piece on me, and I'd be on my way to a jail cell right now instead of taking Seton back with me to my house.

The thought of what he would have done to her if I hadn't been there made my blood run cold in my veins. Something rushed through me, a wave of fierce protectiveness, that I didn't remember ever feeling before for any living thing, except maybe when I was a kid and my mom was in the later stages of the cancer, the chemo ravaging her body until she looked like she weighed no more than a baby bird.

I flashed back to Seton's wide eyes looking up at me as she tried to fight off Wes, the look of desperation and hope as she recognized me, and suddenly it was Seton at nine years old, her unseeing eyes meeting mine as she sobbed for her father.

I wanted more than anything to be the one who made sure no one ever hurt her again.

We arrived on the other side of town, where my neighborhood was. I turned off the highway onto the side street that led toward my place. I had originally gone to the bar to talk to Seton about Cal, to tell her that he'd gone on a run for us, and that everything had gone just fine. But that would have to wait. Right now, all I wanted to do was get her alone, away from everything except just the two of us.

I pulled up the driveway and cut the engine. Seton scrambled off the bike and I waited as she undid the strap on the helmet, pulled it off and handed it to me. I stood and took her hand as I had at the bar, guiding her up the walk to the front door. We hadn't spoken a word since we'd left the bar.

Unlocking the door, I pushed it open and motioned for her to walk through. I barely managed to get the door shut again before I turned her to face me. Reaching down, I cupped her ass and lifted her up until she was straddling me. Her short black skirt had ridden up a little, and the thin fabric of her panties was positioned just achingly right on my throbbing cock.

She gasped, and angled her hips against me so that she was pressing against my hardness. I buried my face in her hair as it cascaded down over my face. "Seton," I groaned, unable to say anything else.

"Grey," she whispered in response, and then her mouth found mine.

I carried her to the bedroom like that, as we continued to devour one another with our mouths. As I walked, she whimpered and thrust her hips against my

155

growing erection, and it was all I could do to not just throw her on the bed and take her right then. But I had other plans.

I lay her down, positioning myself on top of her, and brought my mouth down on hers again in a long, bruising kiss. Her tongue found mine eagerly, and I slowly began to tease her by brushing the straining bulge in my jeans as lightly as I could over the fabric of her panties. Seton whimpered and arched her hips at the contact. I pulled away from kissing her and she opened her eyes to look up at me. They were dark and wide with desire, like two emeralds. Her lips parted, swollen already from my assault on them, and she as we stared wordlessly at one another she pulled her lower lip between her teeth in a gesture that made me so crazy I almost forgot my self-promise to slow down.

I reached down to her panties and skimmed a finger over her crotch as lightly as I could. I watched with a surge of desire as her back arched in response. "You're soaked," I breathed. "You're fucking wet as hell for me."

"Yes," she whispered. "For you."

"Only for me," I demanded.

"Yes," she repeated. "Only for you."

I couldn't hold back any more. I had to have her. I knelt on the floor by the bed and pulled her shirt up over her head, throwing it on the floor, then reached back behind her and unhooked her little lace bra. A groan of desire escaped me as her luscious tits tumbled free. I pulled her toward me, and fisted my hand in her hair. Her head rolled back as I took first one pert nipple into my mouth, then the other, sucking and teasing them to hardness as she gasped and cried out in pleasure. All I could think about was making her come, so I lay her back and pushed her up further on the bed.

I grabbed the waistband of her soaking panties and pulled them off of her. Then I was between her legs, listening to her as I licked and teased, sucking her clit into my mouth, laving her as her whimpers turned to gasps, and her gasps turned into soft, desperate cries. Her breath began to come faster and faster, her hips thrusting up to meet my mouth, and then she was coming, calling my name over and over as she bucked against my tongue. I continued to lick and lap at her juices as she shuddered, drawing out every wave of her orgasm until her sensitive nub couldn't take any more. I slowed, then stopped, kneeling to move back over her, and kissed her long and deep. I knew she could taste herself on me, and it drove me fucking crazy.

When I pulled away to look at her, her eyes were half open, lids heavy with desire. Her lips were puffy and soft from my mouth, and she bit the bottom one again, then gave me a seductive half smile.

"Your turn," she said breathily. She reached down and pulled at the top button of my jeans, undoing it. Silently, I knelt on the bed and she sat up, not breaking my gaze as she undid the rest of the buttons and pushed down impatiently on the waistband. I stood up and let them fall to the ground. She slid forward and before I could believe my fucking luck, she was taking my pulsing cock in her hand, caressing it lightly as I stifled a moan and closed my eyes.

"You're so big," she marveled. "Greyson…"

I opened my eyes to look at her. My cock was directly in front of her mouth and she was looking up at me, the need showing in her stare. I could have come just from looking at her in front of me like that, her soft lips so tantalizingly close to my cock I could almost feel them. Then, slowly, she opened her mouth and licked softly at the head. I threw back my head and groaned. Her face flushed with pleasure and she whispered, her lips touching the sensitive skin of my tip: "I've wanted to do this so much. I've… I've touched myself thinking about it."

"Fuck, Seton…" I groaned, my voice thick with need.

"I want you, Greyson," she whispered. Her mouth opened, and she slowly wrapped her lips around my cock. It was the best fucking thing I had ever felt in my life. The inside of her mouth was like velvet. She kept looking up at me, not break eye contact as she started to slowly bob her head on my shaft. Her tongue swirled around the head of my cock, and I closed my eyes and prayed to whoever was listening that I wouldn't come in her mouth right that second.

My hands moved downwards, tangling in her hair as she sucked me further into her mouth, taking me deeper each time. Her soft moans vibrated against my skin, making me shudder. I felt like I could burst at any moment, and I had to will myself not to lose control before I was ready. "I'm so fucking close, Seton," I growled, barely able to choke out the words in my need. "God, I love fucking your sweet mouth. It's so warm and wet. Feel what you do to me, Seton. Feel how big I am."

She whimpered around me in response, and began to bob faster. It was almost more than I could take, and suddenly I gasped and pulled out before it was too late. A whine of frustration escaped her and I chuckled. "Not yet, sweetheart," I muttered.

I pushed her back on the bed knelt between her legs, positioning myself. I couldn't fucking wait to be inside her. I reached for my jeans to grab a condom, but she stopped me. "I'm on the pill," she whispered, her eyes wide. "Please. I want to feel you. All of you."

Fuck if I didn't almost lose it right then and there. "Seton…" I groaned in protest.

"I trust you. I'm clean," she said without reservation. "If you tell me you are, too, I'll believe you."

I hadn't exactly led the life of a choir boy, but one thing I was fucking careful about was safe sex. I didn't need any little Greysons running around, and I sure as hell didn't need some club whore to give me a disease. I knew I was clean, but I still hesitated. "Seton, I'm clean, but…"

"Then fuck me, Greyson." Her voice was almost a command, and it fucking ended me. She blushed furiously, but then lifted her head and looked me in the eye. "I want to feel you… I need you to fill me up with your come."

I had never heard anything hotter in my life.

I drew her toward me and knelt on the edge of the bed. Almost shaking with need, I took myself in my hand and slid the hot head of my cock against her slick wet center. "Yes!" she cried out softly. "Oh, God, Greyson…"

It was all the encouragement I needed. With the slightest movement of my hips I could manage, I pressed into her just a little bit, stopping as a wave of pleasure washed over me from the sensation of being inside her heat and warmth. I held my breath as I pulled out slightly and then thrust in again, just a little further. Seton rocked her hips toward me, encouraging me, begging me with her eyes to go deeper. I thrust again, and then again, and then I was all the way inside her, and her pussy was gripping my cock so tight I knew it wouldn't be long. I grabbed her hips and started fucking her, as slowly as I could, but soon I couldn't hold back and I sped up, thrusting harder and deeper as I started to climb higher. Seton closed her eyes and moaned, spreading her legs wider to try to get me as deep as possible. Her breathing sped up and I could tell from the flush in her cheeks and the way she was tensing that she was as close as I was.

"Come for me, baby. I want to see you come for me." I reached down with a thumb and lightly caressed her swollen nub, and she cried out and shuddered into a long, racking orgasm, her pussy pulsing around me, gripping me. I thrust once more, twice, and then I exploded, unleashing all my cum inside her in torrents as she called my name. The force of it was so strong that it felt like every cell in my body had exploded.

When I finally managed to slow my breathing and look at her, Seton had opened her eyes and was staring up at me. A playful smile flitted across her lips.

"What?" I managed to ask, cocking my head.

"I needed that," she grinned.

CHAPTER 15

Seton

After Grey made me come for the second time, we lay sprawled across the bed, catching our breath. Grey eventually opened his eyes and caught me looking at him. A single brow went up quizzically.

"What?" he asked.

"I needed that," I grinned at him. He laughed and drew me to him, kissing the top of my head.

"Me, too," he whispered against my hair. He reached over and pulled a blanket over us, and we fell asleep like that, my head lying on his chest, his strong arms around me.

When I finally woke up, it was early morning. The sun was just starting to cast shadows in the room with its soft light. Yawning, I raised my head and looked around me. I realized that in the strange and emotional state of the night before, I had barely noticed my surroundings when we had arrived at Greyson's house. Now, as I scanned the room, I was very aware that I was in his bedroom, his personal space. It was sparse, yet surprisingly appealing, with just the bed, a night table and lamp, a long, low dresser, and an armchair by the window. The room was done in a tasteful array of light grays and dark browns. Slung over the armchair was his cut, and our clothes littered the wood floor around the bed. I thought of the night before and felt my face flush with a mixture of embarrassment and lust.

"What do you think?" Grey asked beside me. I turned to see him staring at me, his hands clasped behind his head.

"Nice," I murmured, nodding my head appreciatively. "Not exactly the seduction bachelor pad I would have expected."

"I don't bring women here," he murmured flatly.

"You brought me here."

Grey didn't respond. I ducked my head back down to his chest, and he put an arm around me. His chin rested against the top of my head. I closed my eyes, and the rhythm of his breathing lulled into a doze. When I woke up a few minutes later, I looked up to see if he was asleep, only to find him looking at me with a lopsided grin.

"What?" I demanded.

"You were snoring," he smirked.

"I was not!" I protested. "I don't snore!"

He laughed and kissed me on the forehead. "Don't worry, babe. It was cute. You sounded like a puppy."

I snorted. "That's not exactly the sexy look I'm going for."

"A puppy with a nice rack?" he offered.

I slapped him on the arm. "That's sick."

"You do have a damn nice rack, though," he said, reaching down to cup my breast.

"Charmer," I say sarcastically.

"Damn straight," he murmured, his lips lowering to my nipple. "I'm a regular goddamn Casanova."

He pulled my areola into his mouth, teasing it to hardness. I gasped at the sensation that shocked through my body at his touch. He reached down between my legs, finding my center, and groaned against my nipple. "Fuck, Seton. You're so wet. You're so wet for me."

He moved on top of me then, and knelt between my legs. His cock was already hard, and he pressed it against the wetness of my entrance, sliding it slowly back and forth across my clit. I moaned and spread my legs apart for him, almost painfully aroused. I wanted to feel him fill me like he did last night, and I drew in a breath in anticipation. Suddenly, he flipped me over, and I was on top of him, straddling him as he lay back, watching me.

"I want to see you make yourself come with me," he said thickly. His eyes were hooded with desire. I needed release so badly I didn't even think to be shy. I reached down and took his cock in my hand, the tip of it glistening with my juices and his precum, and began to slide it against myself, rocking my hips softly against him. The slick friction of it made me moan, and I threw my head back in ecstasy.

"Fuck, yeah," he breathed. "You're so fucking sexy, Seton."

My breathing began to speed up as I increased my rhythm. I was so turned on I knew it wouldn't take me long, but I couldn't slow down, couldn't wait, I needed it so badly. He reached up and teased my nipples with his thumbs and I felt myself coming closer and closer to the edge.

"Tell me what you want," he groaned.

"I need to come," I moaned immediately. "God, your cock feels so good, Greyson, I'm so close…"

I started to close my eyes but he stopped me. "Look at me. I want to see you come."

I locked eyes with him, watching his own desire play across his face. "Come for me, Seton," he urged. "Come for me on my cock." I shuddered and called his name as I flew over the edge, hips thrusting against his cock. Just as I crested the first wave, he changed the angle of his hips and pushed himself inside me. I cried out as another wave of my orgasm washed over me, and I rode him as he thrust underneath me. I heard him roar as he climaxed, filling me with his release.

I collapsed on top of him, and his arms wrapped tight around me. We slept.

When I woke, the sun was up, and the smell of fresh-brewed coffee was wafting toward me. I breathed deeply, smiling, and opened my eyes to find Grey standing at the foot of the bed, a cup in his hand.

"I hope you like coffee," he said. "I don't know how you take it. I've got some sugar, but I don't have any milk or cream."

"Cream and sugar are an abomination," I replied, taking the cup from him gratefully. "Black is the only acceptable way to drink coffee."

"Okay. You're hardcore about coffee. So noted," he grinned.

I took a sip and moaned gratefully. "Thank you. This is heaven."

He sat down on the bed next to me. "I don't really cook, so there's no breakfast."

I propped a pillow behind my back and sat up. "Luckily, I do. Do you have eggs?"

He nodded. "And bread. Cheese, too, I think. Not too much else, though."

"Do you have any vegetables?"

His brow furrowed. "Frozen, maybe."

"Okay," I said. "I can work with that. Just give me a couple of minutes to start feeling human."

After I finished my first cup of coffee, I grabbed my T-shirt and underwear from the floor, saying a silent prayer of thanks that Grey hadn't destroyed that pair like he had the first one. Out in the kitchen, I found cheese in the fridge, and some sliced ham, too, so I made us omelets and toast. Grey made a show of mocking the omelets as too fancy for a big he-man like himself, but I noticed he didn't hesitate to gobble it up after he had taken the first experimental bite.

"Holy mother of God, this is good," he marveled as he chewed.

"Have you seriously never had an omelet?" I asked, crinkling my nose.

"Guys like me only eat food that comes off a bone," he growled, but his eyes were twinkling.

"Caveman," I bantered.

"Seriously, though, of course I've had a fucking omelet," he continued. "But this is goddamn fantastic. Did you seriously make this just with the stuff that you found in *this* kitchen?"

I smiled happily, basking in the compliment. Grey wasn't really the type to be effusive, so I believed he meant what he said.

We sat and munched in companionable silence for a few minutes. Eventually, I asked the question that had been on my mind off and on since this morning. "Were you serious when you said you don't bring women here?" I asked, partly to break the silence, and partly because I was genuinely curious.

Grey took another forkful of food. "I don't *sleep* with women. Sex is sex. I don't like complications."

I looked down at my plate. "Is that what I am? A complication?"

He put his fork down and looked at me. "Honestly? Yes," he acknowledged. "But in your case, the complications have advantages."

My heart skipped a beat. "Like what?" I asked.

"Remember what I said about your rack?"

I giggled. "That's really sexist, Grey."

"Not if I mean it sincerely," he countered. "And believe me, I do." His eyes descended to my chest, his lips spreading into an exaggerated leer. "Particularly when you wear that tight little T-shirt and forget to put on a bra."

I reddened. "Stop that, and finish your breakfast."

Grey stood up. "You want some more coffee?"

"Yes, please!" I held out my cup and he refilled my coffee for me. When he sat down, his face had a more serious cast.

"I meant what I said, though," he said quietly. "You're the first woman to spend the night here."

I knew it was probably only because he felt bad about the shock of what had happened with Wes. I found myself wishing it was more, but I pushed those thoughts away and told myself just to be happy with what I had. The sex last night and this morning with Grey had been... unbelievable. I needed to just be content with that and not wish for things that weren't going to happen.

"So," he continued, interrupting my thoughts. "What are you going to do about the bar?"

I sighed. "Well, I think it's fair to say I probably don't have a job anymore."

"Would you want to go back there, after what that pig tried to do to you?" he asked sharply.

"No," I admitted. "I don't think I could. Even though I'm pretty sure Wes would never dare to touch me again after what you did to him." I looked up at Grey, suddenly afraid. "Do you think he'll press assault charges on you?"

Grey snorted. "That little fuck? He knows he deserved it, and much more. He's too much of a pussy to go to the police. He'd have to answer to the club, and he knows it." He leaned back in his chair and looked at me. "So, what are you going to do now?"

"I'm not sure."

Grey cleared his throat. "You could come work at the clubhouse bar."

I eyed him quizzically. "There's an opening?"

He shifted in his seat. "No, not exactly. But we can always use someone who knows how to pour a drink."

"You don't know that I'm any good at my job," I teased him. "Besides, from what little I've seen of that bar, there's not a big call for a bartender who does craft cocktails."

A bark of laughter escaped him. "You got me there. It'd be mostly opening beer bottles and serving shots of whiskey."

"What about the other club members?" I challenged him. "The ones I've seen look pretty dangerous, and they don't look like they necessarily take no for an answer where women are concerned. Wouldn't it be potentially even less safe for me there than at the Cactus?"

He sat back. "You're not wrong. Except the women who hang around the club aren't the type to say no. But yeah, you'd be safe. No one would dare lay a finger on you if they know you're with me."

"Am I with you?" I challenged.

"Fuck yes, you're with me," he growled. "You're a pain in the ass, sometimes," he continued with a smirk, "But like I said before, you have a certain something that makes you worth it."

His eyes bored into mine, and it was as though he was touching me, the way the heat from them raced through me to my core.

"Grey," I started, my voice cracking with emotion. I took a deep breath and let it out. What he was saying… it was more than I could process. We were together, in his eyes, it was clear. And God, if I was honest with myself, I wanted that. More than anything.

But there was so much that could come between us. The club. My brother. The past. I didn't know how to navigate through all of that. It felt like a minefield was separating him from me.

"So," he asked again. "Will you come work at the clubhouse?"

I smiled and shook my head slowly. "Thanks for the offer, Grey, but no thanks. I think I need to take some time to figure out what I want to do next." I made a mental calculation. I had a fair amount of money saved up, which I had been planning to use to go back to college. But deep down, I knew I just didn't want to do that. I figured I had at least six months of income built up, if I was really careful with my spending. Maybe it was time to take a step back and think about my future as more of a big picture.

Grey didn't press it. But he seemed to have something else on his mind. "Uh, Seton. I actually came to the bar last night to talk to you about something."

I blinked my eyes and looked at him. In all the confusion of the night before, I had forgotten to wonder why he had shown up at the bar in the first place. I nodded at him now. "Okay. What about?"

"I wanted to let you know that I sent Cal and another prospect out on their first run for the club yesterday. With two of my best men. They did just fine. I know you've been worried," he added. "So, I just thought I'd come by and tell you that."

"I saw a gun in Cal's waistband the last time I saw him, Greyson," I countered. "It's hard to feel like things will be fine when I know he'll be carrying."

"It's just a reality, Seton." He drained his cup. "It's a precaution. Lots of people pack. You probably encounter a dozen people or more in the course of a day who are armed and you just don't know it. It would be crazy for me to send a brother out without the ability to defend himself."

"So, it really is dangerous, then. Cal really will be in danger sometimes, if he gets patched in."

"It's not an easy life, Seton," he said seriously. "Hell, it's not always a safe life. I'm not going to lie to you." He looked at me. "But it's a life your brother is choosing."

I considered that. "Do you think he's cut out for it? That he'll be patched in?"

"It's too early to tell," he acknowledged. "But I think maybe so."

"Please, protect him, Grey," I whispered, barely daring to ask. "Please."

"Seton," he said gravely, "I can't protect Cal from everything. I can't protect him from the world, or from his choices. Neither can you. I can promise you that I do everything I can for my club and my brothers. I would die for any of them. They would die for each other." His eyes were serious. "Cal won't have the safest life in the world, but he won't be stuck in a fucking cubicle day after day, either. And he'll have a family in the club. It's a brotherhood. It's a hard life, but it's a good one."

A family. The words resonated in my head. Maybe in a way, Cal was looking for a family he didn't have, I realized. With his father dead and an estranged brother, the only remaining actual family he had was me, and to a lesser extent my mom. There were no men for him to look up to, no men for him to emulate. Maybe Cal was just looking for a family, after all.

Grey noticed that I had grown quiet, and didn't disrupt my thoughts. He stood and took the breakfast dishes away, putting them in the sink. He left the kitchen, and noises from the back of the house told me he was occupied with other things, so I sat and finished my coffee, pensive.

Some time later — I'm not sure how much time had passed — a loud curse interrupted my thoughts. Grey came back into the kitchen fully dressed, his jaw clenched.

"Get dressed," he said through his teeth. "We have to go. Now."

CHAPTER 16

Grey

The blood drained from Seton's face when I told her we had to leave. But to her credit, she didn't waste time asking questions, and I was grateful for that. Without a word, she got up from the table and went to the bedroom. In less than a minute, she was back out in the living room, pulling her hair into a messy ponytail.

I held out my phone and showed her the text I'd gotten from Levi:

Go to the clubhouse ASAP. Something went bad with the run. Will call you

Seton's eyes widened in fear as she read it. She opened her mouth but I cut her off. "I don't know. Best thing we can do is get there right now. Levi's on it. He'll call me when he can talk."

Her face was white as a sheet as I handed her the helmet and she silently got on my bike. I drove like a demon and we were there in six minutes. Levi pulled in right behind us and cut his engine.

"What?" I demanded.

"Drive-by." His eyes were murderous. "At Maisie's."

Maisie's was a local diner the next town over that was friendly to bikers. It was a frequent hangout for the club when we came back from a ride.

I swore. "Who?"

"Trigger and Repo, for sure. The two prospects, too, I think."

Behind me, Seton made a strangled sound.

"What do we know?" I demanded.

"Not much yet. At least one of them had an AR-15 or something like it. Sounds like they might have hit some civilians, too. At least one of ours is wounded. I sent Winger and Moose down there with the van."

"Who got hit?"

"Trigger," Levi responded.

Shit. I nodded. "Okay. Seton, climb off." She scrambled off the bike and almost fell to the ground. Levi caught her as she stumbled. I got off and took her from him, gathering her into my arms. She was trembling like a leaf.

"Seton," I said gently, lifting her chin. "I'm going to take you inside. You'll wait here. Levi and I are going down there."

She looked up at me with tears in her eyes. "Okay," she whispered.

I nodded to Levi to stay there. "Back in a second," I said.

I led Seton inside. Repo's old lady was there, as well as a few of the club whores. "This is Seton," I said to them. "She's with me. You ladies take care of her. One of the prospects is her brother."

Jules, Repo's old lady, nodded. "Come on, honey. You and me'll wait together. My man's there, too."

Seton allowed herself to be led over to an area with a bunch of couches. I leaned in to Jules and murmured, "We'll call you as soon as we know anything."

She nodded and put her hand over mine. "I know you will," she said with a tremulous smile.

Levi was already on his bike when I got back outside. He nodded toward the clubhouse. "That new?" he asked, meaning Seton.

"Yeah." I straddled the bike. "She's Cal's sister."

His eyes widened. "Nice rack," he said simply. I had to laugh.

"Come on, brother," I replied grimly. "Let's do this."

We got to Maisie's about twenty minutes later. Yellow police tape cordoned off the scene. Bullet holes riddled the front of the diner, and paramedics were attending to some of the less wounded people who looked like they had been injured by shattered glass.

We scanned the crowd for familiar faces, avoiding the police officers who were staring at us with a range of curiosity to outright hostility. Levi nudged me and pointed to Repo, who was coming toward us. He had a large gash on his forehead that looked to be from flying glass, but looked to be otherwise okay.

He lifted his chin at us. I strode forward, Levi close behind me, and clapped Repo on the shoulder. "Good to see you, brother. What happened?"

His face was a stony mask. "Fucking assholes with semi-automatics mowed down the place." He looked back toward the restaurant. "Couple civilians are probably gonna be in critical condition, maybe worse."

Goddamnit. The Stone Kings tried hard as hell to keep our business away from the community. "Any idea who it was?"

"Not sure. A witness said the gunfire came from a dark-colored van. Sped through the parking lot, sprayed the place with bullets, then drove away." His face registered a look of disgust. "Our bikes are fucking torched, though, so it's pretty clear we were the targets. None of them are drivable."

"What about the brothers?" Levi cut in.

"Minor injuries. Trigger took the worst of it, a bullet to the leg. Winger and Moose came and got them all with the van, took Trig to see our doc to get patched up."

I breathed a sigh of relief that Cal and the other prospect were okay, and that Trigger wouldn't have to go to the hospital. The less contact we had with the authorities on this, the better. The Stone Kings would settle this on our own terms, once we figured out who was responsible.

"Who else was with you guys?" I queried.

"It was me and Trig and the two prospects," Repo answered. "We got back from the run last night and ended up partying all night at the clubhouse. The prospects are pretty all right, by the way," he grinned. High praise coming from Repo, who was notoriously tough on hangarounds and prospects. "This morning we were pretty raw, so we decided to come out to Maisie's for a hangover special."

"You figure this was the Cannibals?" I asked Levi. "Payback for our run into their territory yesterday?"

"They're fuckin' lunatics, if it was," he spit out. "Why the hell would they let us pass through with no reaction, and then come try to mow us down in our territory later?"

"Lunatics, or cowards," I muttered. Word was that the Cannibals had just voted in a new president after the old one had been killed in a shootout with a rival MC. The new prez's name was Skull, and I didn't know much about him. If this was the Cannibals, it didn't bode well for our future relationship with them, and meant that our territory was in danger of being compromised. Ultimately, this could end up in a war between the two clubs unless something could be done to prevent it. But if this was essentially a shot across the bow from them, it was a pretty clear indication that they didn't intend to be reasonable. I briefly wondered if their new president had some sort of death wish.

"How did you find out about this?" I asked, turning to Levi.

"I called him," Repo answered. "Right after they took off. Shitty service up here, though, the call cut out right after I made contact."

Levi nodded his assent. "All I got was there was a problem, and where they were. So I texted you so we could meet at the clubhouse and ride out together."

"You did the right thing."

"So, what happens now?" Repo asked.

"I'll be fucked if I know," I answered honestly. "Whoever did this is gonna pay, though, and pay hard. First things first, we get an ID on that van. Probably too much to ask that it wasn't stolen, but if we do get a positive ID that it's theirs, that makes the rest of our decisions pretty fucking simple." I looked at Levi. "Get some eyes on it."

"You got it boss." He stepped away and took out his phone.

I turned to Repo. "Your old lady is waiting at the clubhouse for you. You'll want to let her know you're okay." He nodded and stepped away.

I thought about Seton, then. I knew I should call and let her know what happened. It was gonna seem like cold fucking comfort, though, for her to hear that her brother was okay but that he had been in a drive by shooting. I considered the very real possibility that she would be angry enough to break things off with me completely.

I couldn't blame her. Hell, I should be the one to break things off with her, just to protect her from having one more person to worry about whenever shit like this went down. I couldn't allow her to be part of this life, I realized as I walked back to my bike and texted Sag to make arrangements to pick up the bullet-ridden bikes. It wasn't right for me to try to keep her, just because I was in love with her.

Because I was in love with her.

Just my fucking luck.

When Levi returned from his call, I motioned toward our two bikes. "Come on," I said. "Let's get out of here before the cops come over and start asking questions."

Levi nodded, and then suddenly broke into a shit-eating grin. Repo hardly ever smiled.

"What?" I asked, frowning.

"Repo's bike is fucked. He's gonna have to ride bitch," he laughed.

I snorted. "Not my bitch. He's all yours."

Levi wandered over to Repo and said a few words. They came back toward me, Repo glowering and Levi almost jubilant.

"Get on, sweet butt," Levi cooed, patting the seat behind him.

"Fuck you," Repo muttered.

I got a phone call on the way back, and we stopped by the side of the road so I could take it. It was Moose, telling me that Trigger was all patched up, and that the prospects were fine, only some minor scratches. I relayed the info to Levi and Repo, and we finished the ride back to the clubhouse.

When we walked in pretty much the entire club was there waiting for us. The first thing I saw was Seton, who came running over to me, her eyes wide and dark.

"What happened?" Her hands clutched my arm. "Is Cal okay?"

"Cal's fine, sweetheart," I murmured. "Don't worry. He'll probably be back any minute."

She let out a deep breath and tried to smile. "Will you tell me what happened?"

"Eventually." I put my arm around her. "Right now, I need to talk to the men. Why don't I take you home?"

"No," she said stubbornly. "I want to wait for Cal to get back."

I pulled her close and kissed her. "Okay, you win. Stay here for now. I'll take you back later." Detaching myself from Seton, I walked over to Repo and his old lady, who were engaged in a reunion of their own. "Hey," I nodded to them both. Jules smiled tremulously.

Turning to Repo, I said: "When Trigger and the rest of them get back, we need to have church. Don't go anywhere."

"Got it." He looked at Jules. "I could use a beer."

"Don't go anywhere," she smiled. "I got you." She kissed him and wandered over to the bar.

Just then, the door opened. Winger and Moose strode in, followed by Trigger on crutches, and finally, Cal and Frankenstein.

"Hey, what's Frankenstein's actual name, anyway?" I asked Repo.

He grinned. "Chad."

"Fuckin' *Chad*?" I sputtered. "Jesus H., Frankenstein is one hell of an improvement."

"You're tellin' me," he drawled.

We stood around and watched the happy faces as the men were welcomed back. Seton was talking to Cal, her face beaming with relief. I gave them a few minutes, then raised my voice above the din. "Church in three!"

A murmur of assent rose in response. I turned to Repo.

"I want the prospects at this meeting, too."

He gave me a questioning look. Prospects were never allowed in church.

"They were there," I said. "I want them to be part of this discussion. I want to know what they saw."

"I see your point. Probably best to have all the intel we can."

*   *   *

"I say we ride back into their territory and set fire to their fuckin' clubhouse," Moose bellowed loudly. A few of the men voiced their agreement.

I had to admit it was tempting. The tension and anger in the room were palpable. The Stone Kings were out for blood. I looked around the table. "Did anybody who was there see anything that could tell us who it was?" I looked at the prospects. "You?"

Cal looked at Frankenstein, who shook his head. "All I saw was the barrel of an AR sticking out of a van."

Cal agreed. "I didn't see anything either. Fuck, glass and shit was flying all over the place so fast it was impossible to see anything."

"Had to be the Cannibals," Trigger said.

"What's the message?" Repo asked. "Payback for driving into their territory? That makes no goddamn sense, to go out that hard."

"Fuckin' idiotic, doing a goddamn thing like that, with no context and civilians all over the goddamn place, I growled."

"Could have been the Aztecs," Tiny said.

"Nah," Moose countered. "That's not Aztecs' M.O. Besides, we got no beef with them right now. I still think it's the Cannibals."

"What's the message?" Repo repeated.

"Preemptive warning, maybe," Trigger replied.

"Warning about what?"

"Who knows? A giant 'don't fuck with us' message. A blanket statement?"

"Some warning, when they were too much of a bunch of fuckin' pussies to even show us who they were," spat Levi in disgust.

"All right." I nodded at the prospects. "You two. You can leave." They stood and filed out, closing the door behind them.

"Okay." I leaned my elbows on the table and folded my fingers. "Here's how we're gonna play this. We don't know who did this, but the Cannibals are the most likely culprits. Fact is, with them having a new president, we don't know much about how they plan to operate going forward." A change in leadership could alter a lot about the way it operated, for bad or for good. "So we're gonna presume right now that this is the first move in a pissing contest."

"So, how do we piss back?" challenged Moose.

"We get ourselves ready for a battle. Maybe even a war," I announced. "If this is the way they communicate, then negotiation ain't gonna cut it with them." I turned to Levi. "You're gonna go make a recon visit to their clubhouse. See what you can see. See if you can identify the van there. Find out what they're up to. Take one or two of the others with you, your choice."

Levi looked around the table. "Moose. Repo." The two men nodded.

I looked at the three of them. "This is recon only. Not looking for payback. Yet. Got that?" I eyed Moose for emphasis. He scowled, but nodded once.

"Okay." I banged the gavel. "Church is over. Officers, stay behind."

The men filed out in uncharacteristic silence. Trigger, Winger, Levi, Moose and Repo stayed in their seats.

"How you doing, Trig?" I asked.

"Okay," he muttered. "Good thing it's my right leg. I should be able to ride before too long."

"We gonna have to replace the bikes, or can they be repaired?" I hadn't bothered to look closely at them when we were at Maisie's.

"We might be able to save one or two of them," Repo said doubtfully.

"All right. When we bring them back here, we'll see what can be done. Whatever can't be saved, the club will replace." I changed the subject. "How'd the prospects do?"

"They did good," Repo affirmed. "Frankenstein went into action and ducked in behind a booth after the windows got shattered. He fired off a few rounds, probably hit the van once or twice."

Winger grunted. "That's good. Makes it easier to identify, since I'm guessing no one got their plates, if they had any."

"Cal didn't do so shabby himself." Trig said approvingly. "He grabbed a little kid sitting a couple tables over, took him down on the ground and covered him so he wouldn't get hurt."

I nodded. You get a person in a life or death situation, you know more about them from their first reaction than you could learn about them in ten years. Both prospects showed good instincts.

"Okay. Good." I stood up. "We'll talk again when Levi, Moose, and Repo get back."

In the meantime, it was time to go talk to Seton.

CHAPTER 17

Seton

The hours I spent at the club waiting for Cal and the others to get back were the most scared I had ever been in my life. Grey had apparently put the clubhouse on 'lockdown' before he left to go check things out, and so no one was allowed to come in or leave until they got back. A few of the club members stood guard at the doors, and I could hear the occasional murmur of their voices as they checked in with each other, but other than that it was fairly quiet.

I knew that apparently the attack at the diner was over, and that no one in the club was critically hurt. In theory, Cal and the others were out of danger, but all the same I kept thinking about the day of my father's death and how awful it would be to have my brother die in the same way. The irony was, though, that this time, it was the club members who were the victims, instead of my "civilian" father.

And then there was Greyson. I knew that as president, he would be an immediate target of anyone with bad intentions toward the club. Having them both out there was making me frantic, and I only managed to contain myself because Jules, Repo's old lady, made sure I wasn't left alone.

Jules was amazing to me during the wait. She was so patient and kind. She looked to be about thirty, with ash blond hair and blue eyes that twinkled when she talked. She was funny and genuine, and I liked her immediately.

"How do you stand it?" I asked her. "How can you not go out of your mind when things like this happen?" I felt sheepish that her husband (were they married, I wondered abstractly?) was out there in danger, but she was calmer than I was.

"It doesn't get easy, but it does get easier," she assured me. "I trust Repo. I know he can defend himself. This is the way things are. It's better to just accept them and have faith. Your brother's in good hands with the men." She gave me a knowing look. "And don't you worry about Greyson. He'll be fine."

I blushed. Up to now, she hadn't mentioned Grey at all.

"How long you and he been an item, sugar?" she asked. "I haven't seen you around here before."

"I'm not really sure we are an item," I admitted. I thought about what he had said when we came into the clubhouse earlier: *She's with me.* "I mean, obviously, there's something going on between us. I just don't know what it is."

"Well," she drawled, taking a sip of her beer. "I've never seen Greyson Stone look at a woman the way he looks at you. So I think it's a pretty sure bet the two of you are an item."

"He said he doesn't do relationships," I ventured. "I stayed over at his house last night, and this morning he told me that normally he doesn't have women do that."

She erupted into peals of laughter. "Now, that *is* an understatement! Honey, if you've been in the inner sanctum of Grey's bedroom, you can count yourself as one of the lucky few. If not the only." She leaned back and gazed at me speculatively. "I can see what he sees in you. You're a real beauty."

I blushed and looked around the room at the half a dozen other women who were there. Most of them were young and blond, with huge breasts and clothes that looked painted on. "I don't know if I'm in the same category as them," I observed. "Are they 'old ladies,' too?"

She snorted. "Hell no, most of them are just club wh… uh, women who hang around the men, hoping they will take an interest. Jacie, over there," she pointed a finger, "she's Sag's old lady, but," her voice dropped to a conspiratorial whisper, "I don't think she's gonna last."

"You don't sound like you like her very much," I whispered back.

"Eh, she's just a club whore who got lucky," Jules shrugged. "Pardon my French."

Just then, one of the door guards shouted a word to another. The front door opened and Grey stepped in, followed by two other men. I stood up and ran over to him before I even knew what I was doing.

"What happened?" I asked anxiously "Is Cal okay?"

"Cal's fine, sweetheart," he murmured into my ear. "Don't worry. He'll probably be back any minute."

I exhaled all at once. I hadn't even realized I'd been holding my breath. "Will you tell me what happened?"

"Eventually." He put an arm around me, hugging me to him. "Right now, I need to talk to the men. Why don't I take you home?"

"No. I want to wait for Cal to get back." I knew I wouldn't be able to stand it, pacing back and forth in my apartment, waiting for a call. I had to see for myself that Cal was safe.

Grey pulled me close and kissed me. "Okay, you win. Stay here for now. I'll take you back later."

Relieved, I let him go talk to the other men and went back to my vigil with Jules. About half an hour later, the guards opened the door again. A group of men streamed in, one on crutches, and finally Cal. I leaped up with a shout and went to him.

"Oh, my God, Cal, are you okay?" I cried, hugging him.

He seemed surprised to see me. "Yeah, I'm fine, See. Really." He frowned. "But, what are you doing here?"

Belatedly, I remembered that he had no idea that I even knew Greyson Stone, much less that there was anything going on between us. I stammered out the first thing I could think of. "I, uh, met Greyson when you left my car here. He told me what happened and drove me here so I could wait."

Cal didn't appear to be too happy that Grey had involved me. "Uh, okay, I guess," he frowned. "But you could have just waited at your place, Seton. I don't like the idea of my sister waiting here for me to get back." He looked around, embarrassed. "It looks like I'm some sort of little kid. Plus, it's dangerous."

I wanted to tell him about Greyson, I really did. But something held me back. Hell, I didn't even know if there was anything real between us. I thought back to Jules' whispered confidence about Jacie: *I don't think she's gonna last.* For all I know, someone would be saying that about me soon.

"It wasn't dangerous," I retorted, trying to change the subject. "We were on lockdown. The MC had guys guarding all the doors just in case." I contemplated the irony of me assuring him that I was safe.

Suddenly, Grey's voice cut through the chatter. "Church in three!" he yelled.

I looked at Cal. "What does that mean?"

"It means the club's having a meeting in three minutes."

"Oh."

A bearded man wearing a cut with a patch that said "Road Captain" came up to Cal. "Prez wants you and Frankenstein at church."

"Sure thing," Cal said. He turned to me. "I gotta go."

The men were away for a while. I was uncertain what to do. On the one hand, I didn't know whether Grey would be mad that I was still there when they were done. On the other, I didn't have my car, so I would need a ride home if I left. So, I just decided to wait. I struck up some awkward conversations with a couple of the other women, and eventually sat down at the bar and chatted with the blond bartender to make the time pass more quickly.

After a while, Cal came out with a tall, lanky guy with gaunt features who looked to be in his early twenties at most. They approached the bar, and Cal asked for a beer. He didn't look too happy that I was still around.

"Seton," he muttered, "This is Frankenstein." I tried not to laugh at how well the nickname fit him.

"Nice to meet you," I replied, not knowing what you were supposed to say when you met a guy named Frankenstein. He nodded a silent greeting to me.

"So, uh, Seton, you gonna be hanging around much longer?" Cal asked. He glanced around the room nervously.

"I, um, don't have my car," I said, hoping he wouldn't offer to drive me back.

"Huh. Well, I'd give you a ride, but my bike got kind of shot up at Maisie's." He looked at me curiously. "How'd you get here, anyway?"

"Um… Grey brought me," I reminded him.

"Oh yeah." Cal responded with a frown. The words hung in the air awkwardly.

The noise of a door opening in the back made him turn his head, and I looked with him to see Grey emerge with five of the other men. Grey broke apart from the group and approached us, accompanied by the large, muscled man who had caught me when I almost fell off Grey's bike. He was covered in intricate tattoos that adorned all the visible skin from his neck down. Grey spoke to Cal and Frankenstein:

"You two go on out to the garage. Your bikes should be brought back pretty soon. Look them over with Repo, see whether they can be salvaged. If not, the club'll take care of getting you new ones."

"Thanks, prez," Cal said, his tone sincere.

"I'm not your president," Grey retorted, his voice suddenly sharp.

Cal immediately apologized. "I'm sorry, sir," he said in a contrite voice. My eyes widened. This was the second time I'd heard him actually apologize for something with no argument.

Grey softened a bit. "Apology accepted. Now go look at your bikes." He looked from Cal to Frankenstein. "And good job today. You did okay."

Cal and the other prospect left. The large tattooed man looked at Grey. "You need the lockdown to continue?" he asked.

"No, I think the men can stand down for now. Let me know when the recon run is planned. We'll talk about security then."

Tattoos looked at me. "Ma'am," he murmured, then turned and left.

"Who was that?" I asked.

"That's Levi," Grey said. "He's my Sergeant at Arms."

I frowned. "What does that mean?"

"It means he's in charge of safety and security," Grey replied. His arm went around me possessively.

"He doesn't talk much, does he?" I asked. I was a little intimidated by him. He looked dangerous.

Grey chuckled. "No. He's not exactly a ray of sunshine. But he's tough as hell, and when he does talk, you know that whatever comes out of his mouth is important. I'd trust him with my life."

I watched Levi's retreating form with curiosity.

"I should take you home," Grey said suddenly.

My heart sank, and I chastised myself. I didn't know what I had expected — that he would ask me to come back to his place? That I would stay here with him?

I tried not to let my disappointment show. "My car's still at the Cactus from last night," I pointed out.

"I'll have one of the boys bring it to your place," he said. "Give me the key." His eyes twinkled. "I'll have them put it in the side pocket on the driver's side."

I couldn't help but laugh at the reference to how we'd met. "Okay," I said, reaching into my pocket and pulling out the small ring that held my car key and my house key. I detached the former and held it up to him.

"Tiny!" He called out. A short, compact man with long, dark hair came up to us.

"This is Seton. Get this car delivered from the Cactus Bar downtown to her place. Silver Mazda Protege."

I gave him my address.

"Now," Grey said when Tiny had gone. "Let's get you home."

CHAPTER 18

Grey

We didn't say much on the way to her place. Seton seemed so relieved about Cal that I didn't want to do anything to break that feeling, so I just let her snuggle in next to me on the bike and wrap her arms around me. The feeling of her holding on to me for protection, trusting me, worked on me the whole way to her house, and I felt like more and more of a fraud with every mile. By the time I pulled over to the curb outside the address she'd given me, I had made up my mind that it was time to come clean.

Seton climbed off the bike, by now doing it like she'd been doing so all her life. She handed the helmet to me and I hooked it over the back seat after I'd climbed off.

Seton lived on the ground floor of a small, compact duplex with a tiny side yard that boasted a minuscule but well-tended garden.

"Welcome to my place," she said shyly. "You want to come in for a bit?"

I grunted my assent. I wasn't going to tell Seton, but I wanted to make sure the apartment was safe and no one was waiting for her inside. *If you would leave her alone, you wouldn't have to worry that she was safe,* my inner voice reminded me, and I frowned angrily that because of me, Seton could potentially be in danger. I followed behind her cursing myself. I watched with a mixture of desire and frustration the sexy way she swayed her hips when she walked, and watched as she fit the key into the lock on her front door.

We entered the apartment to find a woman of about Seton's age on the couch. She had long, wavy blond hair and a pattern of geometric tattoo sleeves on both arms. She had earbuds in and was listening to something that was causing her to bob her head and smile slightly, her eyes closed as she appreciated the beat.

Seton tapped her softly on the shoulder and she opened her eyes. "Hey," she smiled up at Seton, then turned and looked at me, startled. "Oh, I didn't hear you come in," she said, her voice registering her surprise.

"Carly, this is Greyson," Seton smiled, glancing over at me.

"Grey," I corrected, nodding at her.

The woman raised her fingers in a small wave. "Hey," she breathed, then cut her eyes toward Seton questioningly.

"We're uh, going to go back to my room for a bit," Seton grinned at her shyly.

"Sure thing," Carly replied. Her lips started to curl into a smile, but she suppressed it.

"Come on," Seton said, looking at me seductively through a lock of hair that had fallen into her face.

I followed her back, noting the locations of exits and windows as I went. Seton led me into her bedroom, a reasonably tidy but small space with one wall lined with bookshelves. A double bed with no headboard was shoved against the far wall under a window to make as much space as possible. Seton sat down on the bed and I sat next to her.

"So," I said. "Your room." I was feeling conflicted about being here, but I wasn't ready to launch in to what I wanted to say just yet.

"My room," she agreed. She looked through her hair at me again. I felt myself get hard with desire but forced myself not to do anything about it. She looked momentarily disappointed, but seemed to shake herself out of it. Then she seemed to remember something and her lips curved into a conspiratorial smirk. "You know, Cal was really surprised when he came back to the clubhouse and I was there. I totally forgot he didn't know about us." Her face flushed slightly when she said 'us,' and it made me want to kiss her.

"Huh. Yeah, I imagine that was kind of weird for him," I agreed.

A soft giggle escaped her then. "It feels weird to have you here."

"Weird how?"

"Just…" she blushed, then continued bravely. "I've thought about you a lot when I'm in bed, so… now that you're here, it makes me want to do the things I thought about."

I almost groaned as I felt my dick twitch in response. This was not going the way I wanted it to. I realized I had to get out what I needed to say. Rip the Band-aid off before I pushed her down on the bed and did exactly what she was trying to get me to do.

"Seton," I began, my voice almost cracking with desire. I grabbed her hand and held it. "I need to tell you something."

Her smile faded a little, but she kept her voice light. "What is it?" she asked.

I hated that she was worried what I was about to say would hurt her. I hated even more that she was right.

"It's something… something I should have told you a long time ago."

Her eyes opened wide. "Do you… are you with someone else?"

"No," I growled in frustration. "Fuck, no, Seton. I wasn't lying when I told you there's no one else."

She sat up straighter then. Her smile was gone, and she looked at me bravely, her eyes serious. "What, then?" she challenged.

"I knew about your dad's death. I knew who you were as soon as you said your name," I said. I took a deep breath and looked at her. "Because the person who killed him was my uncle."

A small sound escaped her throat. "Your uncle?" she choked out.

"Yes, my uncle Lawless. My mom's brother was the one who did it. And there's one more thing." I turned to face her. "I was there."

"You... what?" she whispered.

"I was there. I was in the crowd when your father died. I... You looked at me. We looked at each other, when you were on the ground with your father."

It was done. I'd finally told her. All I could do now was wait for her reaction.

If I'd thought Seton would yell at me, or cry, or throw things, I was mistaken. The blood drained from her face, and she looked away from me toward some point on the wall. She slowly, firmly detached her hand from mine. "Go," she said in a strangled whisper. "Just go."

It was what I had wanted, in a way. What my head wanted, anyway. But my heart felt like it was going to burst out of my chest as I stood up, quietly walked to the door, and closed it behind me.

In the living room, Carly's curious gaze met mine. "You leaving?" she asked.

"Yeah," I said tiredly. "Look in on her in a while, will you?"

Without waiting for a response, I left the house, got on my bike, and rode away.

* * *

Back at the clubhouse, I tried to convince myself that drowning myself in pussy was just what the doctor ordered, to convince myself that Seton Greenlee had been nothing special. But my heart just wasn't in it. I pushed away the club whore that was grinding on my lap and grabbed a couple shots of whiskey from the bar.

Eventually, some intel started to come in from the recon mission. The van used in the drive-by hadn't been found, so we assumed it was either in a chop shop somewhere or had been ditched or torched. But Trigger, who still couldn't ride because of his leg, had managed to find out some info by shaking the trees. Turned out, there was evidence the Cannibals had joined the Aztecs cartel. Which was fucking interesting, because we had a truce with the cartel that had allowed us to avoid a turf war for years now. If the Cannibals truly had joined the cartel, and they had been behind the attack that killed Hammer, much less the drive-by, they were breaking the truce. Lupine and neighboring Fox Bluff, where Maisie's was located, were strictly off-limits to them. The potential for this to be a much larger and complicated problem had just reared its very ugly head. Before, the only question was to find out who had been responsible for the drive-by at Maisie's and Hammer's death. After that, the response was clear: justice. Blood. It was a formula I was comfortable and familiar with.

Now, if everything we knew was true, the question was, had the Cannibals committed both of these crimes as part of the cartel? And if so, was the cartel behind it, or were the Cannibals going rogue… or worse, working on a power grab?

These were questions, I knew, that required shifting from a short-term view to playing the long game. The Cannibals, if they were responsible, would taste our vengeance. That part was certain. But what was also clear was that the Stone Kings had to get ready for the possibility of an upcoming war.

In a fucked-up way, I was glad for the distraction from Seton that these new developments presented. I knew it had been the right thing to come clean to Seton, so that she would push me away and I would be forced to forget her. Even though it felt like I was fucking dying inside, I would force myself to shut her out. That was the only form my love for her could take: I had to protect her. The way I felt about her, what I wanted for myself: that was immaterial. Just as I had to put the club's needs before my own in any decision, I needed to put what was best for Seton before my own desires.

And the only way I could do that was to make sure that she stayed far, far away from me.

CHAPTER 19

Seton

Andi had been texting and calling me almost non-stop since the morning after Grey had come to the bar and beaten Wes to a pulp. We hadn't seen each other in several days, in spite of her persistence, and I knew she was worried, even though I had texted her back a couple of times to tell her I was fine.

I hadn't bothered to call in sick for my next two shifts, and I hadn't heard a word from Wes about it. I knew he was afraid to fire me after Grey almost killed him. I also knew I couldn't go back to work at the Cactus after what had happened. In fact, it didn't seem like I could go back to anything in my life. Ever since Grey had told me the truth about who he was, it seemed like everything had screeched to a halt at once. My job was gone, my brother was pulling away from me, and the one man who had ever made me feel like I could trust him — like a real, complete woman — had apparently been lying to me from the very beginning. My father's death, now that I knew Grey's uncle had killed him, rushed back to the front of my mind as though it was yesterday. I couldn't stop thinking about the little boy whose eyes had met mine that day — the boy I had hated so much because I knew he probably had a father to go home to. Little did I know that the reason I didn't have my own father anymore was because of that little boy's flesh and blood. It was like my past and my present had just driven full-throttle toward each other and crashed in a fiery explosion, leaving me with nothing.

For almost a week, I sat in the apartment, rarely leaving, eating, or showering. I didn't answer the phone, I rarely looked at text messages. Mostly, I just lay on my bed and stared up at the ceiling, or sat unseeing in front of my computer screen as old movies I had seen a million times played on mute. Carly had tried to talk to me numerous times, but had eventually given up when I waved her off tiredly, telling her that I was fine, that I just needed to rest.

One afternoon, as I was sitting on the couch, mindlessly leafing through one of Carly's magazines, there was a knock on the door. I contemplated not answering it, but I knew she was expecting a package, so I went to see on the off chance that it was the delivery man. I peered through the keyhole to see Andi on the other side, looking impatient.

"I know you're in there, Seton," she called sternly. "Open the door."

Sighing, I did as she asked. She stood in the doorway, arms crossed. "You scared me, Seton. Don't do that."

"I'm sorry," I said automatically.

"Can I come in?" she asked in a voice that wasn't a question.

"Sure." Listlessly, I stood back from the screen door and let her open it. She came into the entryway and gave me a big hug before I could push her away.

"Seriously, Seton, Don't do that again. You're my friend. Don't make me worry like that," she said fiercely.

I felt a wave of regret and apologized again more sincerely. She let go of me and stepped back. "You don't look so good," she said with a skeptical look, though not unkindly.

"I don't feel so great," I admitted.

She led me over to the couch. "Look, See," she began, her eyes growing dark with concern. "Is this because of what happened with Wes? Because he is a fucking prick, you know that, right? Did he... how far..."

"No," I cut her off. "It's not that. I mean, he tried to..." I couldn't finish the sentence. "But he didn't get very far before Grey stopped him." I winced as I said his name out loud.

Andi looked relieved. "You'll be glad to know that ever since your boyfriend beat him up, Wes has been creeping around the bar like a terrified field mouse. He's afraid to talk to anyone. He won't even look women in the eye, much less leer at them." Andi gave me a satisfied look. "Also, I gave my notice," she announced. "I would have just quit right then, but I felt bad for the servers and other bartenders, so I'm giving that asshole the time to hire someone else. And, I notice he's only been interviewing male bartenders," she said smugly.

I didn't bother to correct that she had called Grey my boyfriend, and gave her a weak smile. "That's great," I said. "But are you gonna be okay finding something else?"

"Oh, yeah," she waved off my question with a flick of her hand. "I actually already got another job tending bar at one of the places our band plays. So, no worries." Andi smiled reassuringly, then looked at me more closely, her brow furrowing. "Seton, honestly, you look like shit. Have you been eating?"

"Not a lot, but I'm okay," I confessed. "I had something to eat yesterday. So far today I've only had some coffee."

"Okay, get up." Her voice turned stern. "You are coming with me."

"Ugh, Andi, I don't want to go anywhere," I pleaded.

"Nope, you don't get to decide," she said, shaking her head. "You're coming with me to Gus's. You seriously need to eat something. You look gray."

Grey…

"You need comfort food. A burger and fries. And then you're going to tell me what's wrong," she ordered. "So, go wash up. I'm starving."

When Andi takes that tone, it's useless to argue with her, so I nodded mutely and hauled myself up the couch. Ten minutes later, I had at least brushed my teeth and pulled on jeans and a tank top. I pulled my hair back into a messy pony and let her lead me out the door to her car. She grabbed some sheet music that was sitting on the passenger seat and threw it in the back so I could sit.

Andi didn't ask me anything else until we had already ordered and gotten our meals. She made me get a burger, fries, and a chocolate malt, most of which I knew I wouldn't be able to choke down.

"Okay," she finally said, after she had personally witnessed me eat a few bites of the food. "If it's not what happened with Wes, what's wrong?"

I knew it wasn't an option not to tell her, after I'd let her drag me all the way here. And frankly, maybe letting it out would help somehow. As much as I didn't want to talk about any of it, I'd been thinking about it nonstop for a week, so it wasn't like saying it out loud was going to bring anything back that wasn't already right there in front of me.

Andi knew that my father had been killed when I was little. She knew that the man who killed him was my mother's lover. But what she didn't know was that he had also been a member of the Stone Kings. And when I told her that Grey was not only his nephew, but that he had been there that day, and had concealed all of that from me, her eyes grew wide with shock.

"Holy shit, See! That's like a soap opera!" Her face reddened. "Sorry, that probably didn't sound very sympathetic. I didn't mean it that way. I mean, it's your life, not a soap opera." She whistled. "But whew! That is crazy!"

"I know." I took a tentative bite of a fry and shook my head. "And honestly, Andi, I feel like *I'm* going crazy. Part of me hates him for this: that he didn't tell me, that all this time he knew, and thought, what, that I would never find out? Like I wouldn't care? I don't know *what* he was thinking!" I closed my eyes, all my emotions flooding to the surface.

Andi reached over and patted my hand. "And the other part of you?" she prodded.

"The other part of me… is in love with him," I whispered.

She nodded. "That's what I kind of got," she said gently. She sat for a moment, and then continued. "How did you find out about his uncle and your dad?"

"He told me. The day after the thing with Wes."

"But he did tell you, of his own volition?" Her brow furrowed. "You didn't have to find out on your own?"

"No," I admitted.

"Seton," she said, leaning toward me, her elbows on the table. "Imagine how hard it might be to tell someone something like that. I mean, 'My uncle killed your father and I saw it happen' is not exactly an easy conversation to have." She peered at me. "Do you think he knew it when he met you?"

"Not exactly." I thought back to the day we met, to how abruptly his attitude shifted when I told him my name. "I don't think he recognized who I was until he heard my last name was Greenlee."

"Well, I have to tell you, I guess I don't one-hundred percent blame him for not bringing up something that was so traumatic for you," she answered. "I can only imagine how hard it would be to tell you a member of my own family had done something so horrible to yours." Her eyes locked on mine with a knowing smile. "Especially if I was in love with you."

I scoffed. "He's not in love with me."

"Seton." Her voice was sharp. "The expression on that man's face as he led you out of the Cactus after what Wes did? The fury in his eyes? That was the expression of a man protecting what was his." She sat back. "You tell yourself whatever you want, but he's in love with you."

I was silent. Was it possible Andi was right? I thought back to everything that had happened between Grey and me. How he had told me I was the first woman to stay the night at his place, to sleep in his bed. How he had almost killed a man who had tried to hurt me. How he always made sure that I was fully satisfied before he took his own pleasure. I could barely allow myself to believe it might be true.

"How did you react when Grey told you?" Andi persisted, interrupting my thoughts.

"I was furious," I admitted. "I kicked him out."

"And you haven't seen him since?"

"No," I said miserably.

"See." Andi reached over and put her hand over mine again. "He's not gonna come looking for you. He's gonna respect your wishes. Hell, he probably feels terribly guilty about it all, and terrible for not telling you sooner." She looked me in the eye. "If you want him back, you need to go to him."

In the days that followed, I spent a lot of time weighing what Andi said in my mind. Damn her, she was always so smart and reasonable, I couldn't help but consider things from a different point of view, even though my gut wanted to continue to hate Grey for deceiving me. The more I thought about it, the easier it was to imagine things from his perspective. Instead of hating the little boy of the past for not losing his father that day, I began to feel compassion for him for seeing a man killed in front of him and knowing his uncle had done it. The memory I had of the expression on young Grey's face, which I remembered so well despite it being so many years ago, looked less curious and detached, and more shocked and afraid. I recognized the wide, wild-eyed stare that locked on mine as one of fear and dread. And now, fifteen years later, two children that had been caught up in a world of violence finally found connection and solace in each other's eyes.

Grey, I had finally come to realize, was not what I had assumed him to be. As a child, I believed him to be just a curious witness to my family tragedy. As an adult, I had taken for granted that a man who was a member of a motorcycle club would be just another unreliable man who would use me and let me down. Yet this man, whose hard, rough exterior would lead most people to believe he could not be trusted, was in truth the kindest, most responsible man I had ever met.

I thought back to what Andi had said that day at the restaurant. If I wanted him back, I needed to go to him. Which, I decided, was exactly what I was going to do.

CHAPTER 20

Grey

It had been over two weeks since Seton had ordered me out of her life, and I was doing a piss-poor job of getting over it. I had tried to drown my sorrows in booze, then in pussy, but nothing worked. I was in such an angry mood that I noticed people starting to shy away from me. Club whores who used to come and flirt with me now eyed me silently and moved away when I walked by.

It was for the best, I knew. Hell, it was what I wanted. I was no good for Seton. This life was no good for her, either. Club life was dangerous, and she deserved better. I knew deep down that the reason I'd had such a hard time telling her about my uncle and her father was because she would be right to be pissed off that a Stone

King was responsible for Clayton Greenlee's death. Her anger at that, and her fury that I had kept it from her, were blessings in disguise. The look of hatred in her eyes, the memory of the pain I had caused her, were what I had needed to make good on my vow to stay the fuck away from her forever.

But goddamn if it didn't hurt like hell.

I tried to focus on club business to keep Seton out of my mind, since whiskey and women weren't holding my interest. I had decided to send word to the new president of the Cannibals, Skull, requesting a meet-up at a secure location. The time had come to meet him face to face, to try to read what was in his mind.

I planned to take five men in with me, plus a handful of others, including the prospects, to mount a guard outside the warehouse where the meet was. Both Cal and Frankenstein were getting handier with their guns, and the possibility of an upcoming war made it more of a priority to test them and make sure they had the balls and the guts for the kinds of work they'd be facing as Stone Kings. I was in the chapel making arrangements with Trig, who would be on crutches for another week or so, when Levi knocked at the door and stuck his head in.

"Boss, there's someone here to see you," he grunted.

"Who is it?" I tossed back, irritated at being distracted from our work.

"The woman you..." He stopped, then tried again. "That woman."

No other words were necessary. I knew who he was talking about, of course.

There was no other woman.

"Fuck," I bit out. "Goddamn it, son of a bitch." I took a deep breath, then let it out slowly, trying to ignore the fact that my heartbeat had just doubled.

"You want me to leave you two alone?" Trig asked, cocking a brow.

"No," I retorted. "I don't want to meet her in here. I'll go out to the bar. You keep working on the plans."

I strode outside, determined to keep this as short as possible. Out in the bar, Seton was waiting for me, and when she saw me her face broke into a smile that almost shattered my heart. She looked fucking beautiful. She had on a light pink sundress. I had never seen her in a dress before, and the combination of sexy innocence felt like it was going to end me. Her chestnut hair hung down to her shoulders in soft waves. Her hands were clasped in front of her nervously.

"Hi," she said softly as I walked up.

"Hi," I said back, as coldly as I could muster. Her face fell a bit, but she drew herself up a little taller and tried again.

"Could we talk for a few minute?" she asked.

"So talk," I retorted, shrugging my shoulders. I crossed my arms in a show of impatience.

Seton's brow furrowed in confusion and I could see her falter. My heart literally ached as I watched her. It was all I could do not to take her in my arms and whisper that I was sorry, that I loved her, that I wanted nothing more than to be with her. But I couldn't do it. If I really loved Seton, there was only once choice. And I was making it.

She looked around the bar nervously and said in an almost-whisper: "Could we talk somewhere more private?"

"Fine." I turned on my heel, not waiting for her to follow, and stomped back to one of the apartments we keep available for unexpected late nights and the occasional visitor. I walked through the door and threw myself on the couch by the window, not waiting for her to sit. "What?" I demanded.

"Grey…" she pleaded. "Why are you being so mean?"

"We're done, Seton," I barked at her. "You know it, and I know it. Your kicking me out was just the final straw. You shouldn't have come here."

"But Grey." Her eyes began to fill with tears, and I could see her trying not to let them spill over. "I… I came to tell you I'm sorry for that night." She sat down on the edge a chair adjacent to me. "I was just so shocked at what you'd told me. I was upset, and didn't know what I was saying." She leaned forward, her eyes imploring me. "I know it's not your fault, what happened to my father. And I know it isn't the club's fault, either." She shook her head. "It was just one man, who had an affair with one woman, and my father got caught in the middle." She looked at me now, her eyes shining. "I remember you, you know. I remember your eyes from that day, looking into mine. Yours was the one face in the crowd I saw. That I still see, all these years later. At the time I hated you for being a witness to it. But now… now I think it makes me feel better that you were there. Greyson," she whispered. "I love you."

It was as though someone had taken hold of my insides and was ripping them out of my body. I had never said I love you to anybody in my life except my mother, and I ached in a way I could never have imagined with the need to say it to her now. Seton was everything I had ever wanted in a woman, and I hadn't even known it until now, when it was too late.

But then again, it had always been too late.

"No," I snarled. I stood up and began to pace. "No. Get out, Seton."

"But Greyson," she cried, her voice determined. "I know you feel something for me. I know it! You can't just deny everything that's happened between us."

"It doesn't matter," I yelled before I could stop myself. "It's not safe for you here! This life, it's not for you, Seton. You're not cut out for it."

Seton blinked, and her eyes went wide for a moment. Slowly, she stood, and in a voice that was almost impossibly calm, she said: "Don't you think I should be the one to decide that?"

"No! I shouted. "Fuck, Seton. You have no idea what you're even saying! You've been to college! You should be, I don't know — working in an important office somewhere, married to a guy who wears a suit to work! You're not some club member's old lady!"

"I wouldn't be 'some club member's old lady'," she remarked, daring a tiny, hopeful smile. "I'd be the president's old lady."

"Goddamnit, no!" I thundered. Her face fell. "No, Seton." I motioned at the door. "Get out. Now."

Her eyes filled again, this time with angry tears. Furiously, she brushed them away with the back of her hand. "You hypocrite!" she cried. "How dare you!" I blinked at her in surprise, and she nodded. "That's right! You're a fucking hypocrite! When I came to you and asked you to kick Cal out of the club, you told me I needed to let him make his own decisions. That he was an adult. And yet *you*! First you lie to me about your uncle and don't give me the chance to decide for myself whether it mattered, and now you tell me the truth, but you don't give me the chance to decide for myself whether I want to be with you. Why the fuck is that your decision and not mine?"

Seton strode forward towards me, fury in her eyes. She stopped not a foot from me, locking her gaze onto mine. "Tell me you don't love me!" she challenged. "Say it, if it's true! But don't fucking lie to me! I deserve better than that!"

I couldn't meet her gaze. I wanted to say it, but I just couldn't.

I looked away. "Just go, Seton," I said quietly.

"You fucking coward," she whispered. A single sob escaped her. Anger welled up inside me, but I pushed it down, knowing that she was trying to provoke me into doing something, anything. I stood there, rigid and silent, as she turned and fled, sobbing, from the room.

It was done. All over. The hardest fucking thing I had ever done in my life. I sank back down on the couch and reached into my pocket for a cigarette. I noticed my hands were shaking.

I knew that from now on, the eyes that would haunt me wouldn't be those of the little girl who had just lost her father. They would be those of the woman whose heart I had just shattered.

CHAPTER 21

Seton

If it had hurt badly to push Grey away, it hurt a million times worse to be pushed away by him.

After I left the clubhouse, I drove aimlessly and recklessly for what seemed like hours, crying and screaming and pounding my fists on the steering wheel. When I ran a stop sign and almost hit an old lady trying to cross the street, I pulled over in a strange neighborhood and cried some more. I cried until my throat was parched and my voice was reduced to a raspy, laryngitic scrape.

It was dark by the time I got home. Carly came in sometime later and found me on the couch, staring into space with the lights off. She was so alarmed by how I looked that she threatened to call Cal, but I made her promise not to. The thought of him potentially mentioning this to Grey was more than I could bear.

In the days and weeks that followed, Carly played nursemaid. She made sure I ate, forced me to bathe once in a while, and called Andi in for backup. They would prop me up in front of the TV and I'd pretend to watch movies with them as they passed containers of ice cream or popcorn back and forth.

I noticed they studiously avoided romantic comedies.

In the end, though, life has a way of forcing you back into it. I don't know if it's true what they say, that time heals all wounds, but at least time creates scabs over the wounds. Otherwise we'd bleed to death. So, one day, about six weeks after Grey had pushed me out of his life, I got up, brushed my teeth, put on clothes, and sat down at the computer to look at employment openings.

Like I had told Grey during better times, I knew I needed to move on from bartending and start thinking about the future. I had been throwing around the possibility of cooking for a living. Enough people had told me that I was a good cook that it had planted a seed in my mind. And cooking was something I had always truly enjoyed. I contemplated going to cooking school, but I wasn't sure that being in a classroom was what I wanted right now. In the end, I found a listing for a place in town that was advertising for a culinary apprentice. I jumped at the chance to apply, and when I actually got called for an interview I could hardly believe my luck.

I showed up at The Mockingbird nervous as hell and expecting to be shot down and possibly even laughed out of the restaurant. I told myself that this was just a practice interview and that I needed to have low expectations, but as soon as I stepped through the doorway, I was struck by an almost desperate desire to work there. It was an elegant yet simple place, with a polished zinc bar reminiscent of pictures I had seen of Parisian restaurants. There were two separate areas, a dining room that looked to be where they served the more elegant fare, and the bar area, which I could tell from taking a peek at the menu served a scaled down, simpler selection of the food in the restaurant. It was beautiful without being overstated, and somehow, I could feel myself being comfortable and at home here.

The restaurant wasn't open for business for the day yet, so it was fairly deserted up front except for a woman rolling silverware into cloth napkins. I took a few deep breaths to calm myself down and walked through.

"Hi, I'm here to see Jillian Kramer?" I said. "I have an interview."

"Oh, sure!" the woman said, standing up from her work. "Hold on a sec, and I'll get her for you." She motioned toward some tables by the front windows. "You can go have a seat over there. That's where she usually does interviews."

A few minutes later, a woman wearing a crisp white T-shirt and dark pants came out. She was tall, with short, salt and pepper hair that looked prematurely gray. She wore no makeup, and no jewelry except for a single gold band on her ring finger.

"Hi, I'm Jillian," she said with a wide smile, extending her hand. I took it, and her shake was firm and no-nonsense.

"Hi, I'm Seton," I smiled back. I was grateful that she at least seemed approachable. Maybe I'd manage not to be so nervous that I made a fool of myself.

She explained the concept of the restaurant, which was primarily about the best locally-sourced food available, great service, and modest pricing without affecting quality. It was modeled on the French brasserie concept, to serve simple but well-prepared food. I nodded as she explained aspects of the menu, and asked a few questions about preparations of some of the dishes so she would see that I wasn't a total idiot. She took me on a tour of the restaurant and the kitchen, and introduced me to a few of the people busily chopping, mixing and prepping. As we went around, she asked me questions about my preferred ways of preparing certain cuts of meat and fish, and meals I'd found memorable and why.

When we came back to the table by the window, she motioned for me to sit down again. She leaned forward, her chin resting on her fist, elbows on the table. "So, Seton. I see you've waited tables, and that you've been a bartender, but you've never worked in a kitchen. What led you to apply to this job?"

"That's true," I admitted. "I've been cooking practically my whole life, though." I took a deep breath and decided to tell the truth. "My mom wasn't around much, so I ended up cooking for my little brother a lot. I'm entirely self-taught, but I guess it's always been an obsession of mine. Cooking is what I do to relax. To meditate, in a way. I love when everything falls away and it's just about the food, and the preparing of it." I thought for a moment, then continued. "I'm at a turning point in my life right now. I went to college for a while a few years ago, but I couldn't figure out what it was I wanted to do. A few months ago, my brother said something to me that made a light bulb go off in my head, and since then, I slowly began to realize that the reason I hadn't gone back to college was because what I wanted to do for a living was cook. I considered going to cooking school, but honestly, I'm more interested in learning on the job. This apprenticeship position is the first one I've applied for, and it's my first choice. If you don't hire me, of course, I'll apply other places, but I love what I've seen here, and I really hope you will."

Jillian leaned back and grinned at me. "I like that answer. Frankly, Seton, your lack of experience put me off quite a bit at first, but I thought I'd take a chance and interview you anyway. I figured either it would be a total waste of my time, or you'd be something special. I think it's the latter. You have the job. When can you start?"

I resisted the urge to jump up and do a happy dance, but just barely. "Any time," I said with a grin that almost split my face open. "Absolutely any time."

I walked out of that restaurant feeling happy for the first time in what seemed like forever. It was almost eery how foreign of an emotion it seemed, like walking off of a plane into a completely different climate from the one you had left behind. The ache of losing Grey was still there, and I knew it would come rushing back, just like it always did. But, for just a moment, it was amazing to feel almost normal again.

On the way home, I stopped by the side of the road and texted Andi and Cal my good news. Andi's response was almost immediate, and she sent me a congratulations text filled with all sorts of party emojis. Cal texted back a few minutes later with a simple, "Congrats sis!!" He stopped over unexpectedly later that night, while Carly and I were celebrating with a bottle of wine, and told me that the vote on him getting patched into the club would be soon, and that he thought he would get in. I told him I was happy for him, and changed the subject before he could see my mood change. Cal had been worried about me lately, but unlike Andi and Carly, I hadn't told him what was wrong. I didn't want for him to know that Grey and I had been together. I knew it would just make it worse to watch Cal awkwardly try not to talk about him or the club for fear it would upset me.

But that night, after Carly had been picked up by the guy she was seeing to go out clubbing, Cal stuck around. We sat on the couch and chatted about my new job, avoiding discussing the MC as much as possible. As we talked he grew increasingly quiet, and I finally got frustrated enough to ask him what was up.

"See," he began. "Can I ask you something?"

A tiny alarm bell sounded in my head. "Sure," I said uncertainly.

"Is there something going on with you and Grey Stone?"

My lip trembled but I managed to control my voice. "No," I said truthfully. "There is nothing going on between me and Grey."

Something in my tone must have told him more than I wanted to. "But there *was* something going on. Wasn't there?" His voice was gentle, and it almost made me cry.

"Yes," I answered, my voice finally breaking. I took a deep breath to calm myself, then continued. "But it's over. It never should have happened in the first place."

"Do you believe that?" His expression was disbelieving.

"Yes," I croaked out. A tear slipped down my cheek, and I brushed it away. "I do."

He sighed. "You know," he began, "Grey's a good man." I opened my mouth to tell him to stop, but he held up his hand and continued. "He is. I know he can seem rough. But I respect the shit out of him. Probably more than any guy I know. And I know he'd be good to you. It seemed weird when I first thought about you and him together," he grinned. "But the more I think about it, it fits." He looked at me with a seriousness I almost never saw in my little brother. "I think you should go for it."

Another tear ran down my cheek. "Cal, Grey rejected *me*. Not the other way around." My voice broke, but I continued. "I went to see him. I told him how I felt. He told me to leave."

Cal scoffed. "Aw, he's just trying to protect you," he responded. "Wait him out. I bet he'll come around."

I shook my head. "It's not going to happen," I told him. "It's been weeks. It's been too long."

"Wait him out." Cal repeated. "Trust me. You guys should be together. You'll figure it out eventually."

He leaned over and pulled me into a one-armed hug. I lay my head on his shoulder. "I doubt it, Cal, but thanks anyway."

"Don't mention it," he replied cheerfully.

"Cal… How did you figure out there was something going on between Grey and me?"

He grinned. "Grey has been one broody son of a bitch lately. It started about the same time you lost your shit. Eventually, even someone as emotionally dumb as I am had to figure it out."

About an hour later, Cal took off, congratulating me again on my new job. We didn't mention Grey again. As I watched him drive away, I thought to myself how easily and simply he had accepted the idea of my relationship with Grey. I promised myself that from now on, I would learn from him and let him make his own decisions, without trying to interfere or make them for him.

My little brother, an adult. Go figure.

CHAPTER 22

Grey

The meet was at an abandoned railroad freight depot close to the edge of Aztec cartel territory. There were five Cannibals present, but more motorcycles than that, so we knew some of them were watching, armed, out of our sight. Some of our men were concealed in the hills, as well, but I brought others to station themselves within the Cannibals' sight.

Four of the five men stood in a line behind the fifth, whose patch indicated he was the president. If that hadn't been an indication that this was Skull, I wouldn't have needed any more clues than his large shaved head, the angular bone structure of his face clearly the reason behind his road name.

"Our friends, the Stone Kings," he called to us in slightly accented English. "So nice to finally meet you."

Five of my men, including the two prospects, stayed back, weapons lowered. I approached with my officers, Trig just behind me. This was his first time out on the bike since his injury, and he walked without a limp, though I knew it was costing him pain-wise.

"Skull," I acknowledged with a chin nod.

"And you are Grey Stone. I am happy to make your acquaintance." He turned his head slightly, indicating the others behind him. "And so are my men."

"As are we." Niceties over, I got to the point. "We hear that the Cannibals are part of the Aztecs cartel now."

"Yes, yes," Skull acknowledged with a smooth, toothy smile. "We decided that the benefits were too great to pass up."

"You may have heard," I continued, eyeing him closely, "that there have been two recent attacks on the Stone Kings."

His eyes widened as he pretended to think. "Oh, yes, I believe I had heard that." He clicked his tongue against his teeth. "Most unfortunate."

I nodded. "Yes. Most." I glanced at his men and raised an eyebrow. "The Cannibals wouldn't happen to have had anything to do with them, would you?"

Skull's grin widened as he shook his head. "Of course not! The Stone Kings have a truce with the cartel. We would never do anything to harm that relationship!"

"I see." I turned my eyes back to the men standing behind him and gave them each a cold, calculating stare, one after another. They all stood straight as military, hands clasped in front of them, their faces stony. "So. We've established that the Cannibals weren't involved," I said, with just a hint of sarcasm. "Would they happen to know anything about who was?"

"I'm sure we do not," Skull intoned solemnly. "Word of honor."

A sharp bark of a laugh escaped me. "Word of honor," I repeated. "Well. In that case. Thank you for your time." I turned to go, then took a step back toward him. "Congratulations on your new position. Do tell the Aztecs hello for me. And let Lalo know we met."

"Of course, of course," Skull nodded, spreading his hands wide. "I look forward to continuing our friendship with the Stone Kings."

I turned on my heel, and walked away, my men following a few steps behind me, with the exception of those who were standing guard. "What do you think?" Trigger muttered under his breath as we walked away.

"I think everything out of that fucker's mouth is a steaming pile of shit."

We arrived at the bikes, and I signaled to Levi to call the men concealed in the trees and tell them to cover the Cannibals until we were out of sight. I turned back toward Trig. "Skull knew about the attacks, that's clear. I'm betting the Cannibals were behind the attacks, but we still don't know why."

He grunted his agreement. "That asshole sure has a fuckin' punchable face," he said, holding his hand out and flexing it a few times.

I laughed and clapped him on the back. "You may well get the chance, brother."

The ride back to town was uneventful, and it gave me some time to collect my thoughts. We were playing the long game, I reminded myself. I still didn't know what the fuck Skull was up to, but I was pretty sure whatever it was, Lalo didn't know about it. Lalo and I had a good working relationship. As much as I could trust an outlaw who wasn't a Stone King, I trusted him. That being the case, I was pretty sure the meet we just had would cause the Cannibals to lay low for a while. In the meantime, I made a mental note to have a face to face with Lalo very soon.

Back at the clubhouse, Trig and I debriefed with Levi and Repo. All of us were of the same mind regarding Skull and the Cannibals. Business done for the moment, and feeling the need to decompress, we wandered out to the bar and Trig and I grabbed a bottle of whiskey to share. But the moment the fiery liquid hit the back of my throat, I found myself thinking about how its color was sort of like the color of Seton's eyes. My mood soured instantly, and I glowered into the glass before setting it on the table with a loud bang.

Luckily, Trig didn't seem to notice, or else he thought my sudden change of mood had to do with the Cannibals meet. "Hey," he said conversationally, "Seems like it's getting about time to be making some decisions about the prospects."

"Yeah," I nodded, trying not to think about Cal as Seton's sister. "What's your take?"

"I vote yes on both of them," he said. "Frankenstein's a good, solid guy. He's not the most talkative, but everything I've seen about him points to him being a good Stone King. Fucker doesn't seem to have a lick of fear in him."

"What about Cal?" Cal had been assigned to drive Trig around while his leg was healing up, so they'd spent a fair amount of time together lately.

He grinned. "Couldn't do better. Pig had a good instinct about him." Pig was Cal's sponsor, the one who had brought him in as a prospect. "Like the fuckin' son I never had, that one."

"You'd chase pussy with your son?" I ribbed him.

"Damn straight," he grinned. "And I told you before. I don't chase pussy. Pussy chases me."

I laughed, and agreed with him that it was about time we put the prospects up to a vote. Trig took a shot of whiskey, then poured another and went to talk to Cal, who was across the room with Repo and Frankenstein. I watched them as Trig spoke to Cal, and then Cal's grin as Trig slapped him on the back. Cal glanced over toward me, and I nodded once at him. Then I sat back in my chair, took a shot of my own, and got lost in my own thoughts.

A few minutes later, a throat cleared next to me. I looked up to see Cal standing beside the table. He looked nervous.

"Grey, can I talk to you for a second?"

I scowled and almost told him to go to hell. Even though I was pretty sure he'd be patched in with no problems, he wasn't a Stone King yet, and prospects as a rule didn't speak until they were spoken to. Especially not to the club president. Sensing my anger, he hurriedly continued. "I know I'm not supposed to do this, but it's not about the club. It's about See."

At the sound of her name, my stomach leapt into my throat.

"What about her?" I said through clenched teeth. I stood up until I was towering over him, fairly daring him to continue. As far as I knew, Cal had no idea there had been anything between Seton and me. The only reason I let him continue speaking was because I was scared something had happened to her. I loved Seton too much to let her get involved with a man like me, but I would do anything protect her. To the death, if I had to.

"Well..." Cal murmured. His eyes flicked away from mine nervously, then back again with a look of resolve. "I asked Seton the other day whether you and she... whether there was something going on between you. She said no, but that there had been."

Goddamnit. I did not want to be having this conversation at all, let alone with a fucking prospect. "What's your point?" I asked, my voice a warning.

"Sir," he began, taking a respectful step back. "I've seen her and you both the last couple of months. You're both... well, excuse me for saying this, sir, but you're both miserable." His eyes, which had been cast downward, now met mine. "I'm sorry. I know I'm out of line. But she's my sister, and I love her. I want her to be happy. And," he paused. "I think she was happy with you."

"She's not cut out to be the old lady of a biker," I declared flatly.

"Is that why you sent her away?" he asked.

I gave him a warning look and flinched. "That's none of your goddamn business."

"I know," he acknowledged. "But... don't you think that she gets to choose that for herself?"

He couldn't have known that that was exactly what Seton had said on our last day together. The words sliced into me as I remembered her stricken face, and the way she had called me a hypocrite. And she hadn't been wrong. Here was Cal, on the verge of becoming a member of the Stone Kings, and I had told her he needed to choose for himself what was right. As for Seton, I had chosen for the both of us, and Cal was right. We were both fucking miserable.

I told Cal he'd said his piece, and that the conversation was over. He didn't argue, and went back to do more shots with the other men. But his words had had their effect. That night, as I sat outside on my back deck, staring out into the darkness, I made my decision.

I would go see her. I would.

But not yet.

I'd give her time to get over me. To move on with her life. So she could really choose.

Then, after that, if she still wanted me…

I'd never let her go again.

CHAPTER 23

Seton

Three months of working at The Mockingbird had flown by as swiftly as the namesake of the restaurant. Jillian was a genuinely nice person, but she was a strict task-master and took her role as my mentor seriously. As I hadn't had any formal training, much of my day was spent doing food prep, such as peeling potatoes, cutting up vegetables, cleaning and disinfecting work stations, and the like. It was boring, repetitive, and sometimes even backbreaking work, and to a lot of people it probably sounded like torture, but I loved practically every minute of it. I loved being in the kitchen. I loved the noise, I loved the speed and the gruff camaraderie among the kitchen staff. Most of all, I loved the learning, both from Jillian's direct instruction but also through osmosis. It was amazing just being there to watch how she ran her kitchen, how she guided and pushed her staff to make the restaurant the best it could be.

And I was usually so busy at work that I barely had time to think about Grey while I was there.

In many ways, The Mockingbird had become my refuge. I came home from the restaurant exhausted most nights, threw myself into bed, and slept a mercifully dreamless sleep. There was something cleansing about the physical exhaustion, so much easier to assuage than the emotional exhaustion I was trying to flee. I knew that at least from the outside I seemed to be doing better, because Andi and Carly didn't look at me with the same sharp, probing gaze of concern. They were watchful still, but seemed more or less reassured that I was on my way to recovery. I was careful to smile and laugh around them, to make casual conversation, and to do the things that we had always done together. But if they didn't know it wasn't the same, I did. The pain in my heart and soul had lessened, but it was still there, throbbing and thrumming like a deep wound trying to heal itself.

Cal had been patched in as a member of the Stone Kings, and though he texted and called me on a regular basis, I didn't see him all that much. In the past, that might have bothered me, but I sensed that he was staying away because he didn't want to remind me of what he knew I was trying to forget.

One evening in late September, just as the weather was beginning to turn cooler at night, I came home after an afternoon shift that had gone on longer than anticipated. As usual, I was fairly tired, and looking forward to a quiet evening sitting on the couch, maybe enjoying a glass of wine and a movie with Carly. I blame the fatigue for the fact that I didn't notice the low-slung motorcycle parked across the street from our duplex, which I drove right by as I swung into the driveway.

The front door was open, so that the air of one of the last temperate nights could pass through. I swung the screen door open and stepped through, gratefully unloading my duffel bag on the floor. I smiled at Carly, who was sitting on the couch staring at the television screen.

"Hey," I greeted her. "Glad you're home. Wanna open a bottle of wine and watch crappy TV?"

She looked up at me then, and I noticed her expression was off. Arms crossed, her brows knit into a frown, she definitely seemed unhappy about something.

"You have a visitor," she said.

Her words didn't quite register. "Huh?" I asked, putting my hands to my back and stretching.

"You have a visitor. In your room."

For some weird reason, my first thought was that she had gotten me a kitten or something, but obviously she wouldn't be looking like she wanted to slap someone if that was the case. I opened my mouth to ask her to explain, but as I did, an awful realization hit me.

My face drained of color. "Grey?" I whispered.

"You should know that I told him to fuck off and die, but he begged me to hear him out." Her frown deepened into a glower. "I don't know if I did the right thing. I'm still sitting here kind of pissed at myself. But," she paused, "I think maybe you should go listen to what he has to say."

My first reaction was to flee. *If I ran out the door right now and drove away*, I thought irrationally, *I don't have to do this.* It had been too long, I had fought too hard to forget him. I wasn't sure I'd survive having to do it a second time. My stomach churned, and for a moment, I thought I might be sick.

I stood for a few moments, my body feeling paralyzed. Then, almost without knowing that my brain had sent any signals to my legs, I was moving toward the bedroom as if someone else was controlling them.

When I got to the door, Grey was sitting on my bed, elbows on his knees, his head hanging, looking at the floor. I cleared my throat and he looked up. His cool blue eyes met mine, and a sob almost escaped my throat. Everything I'd tried so hard to forget, all the emotions I had fought to leave behind me — all of it came surging back like a tidal wave. I stood rooted to the spot, afraid that the slightest movement would be all it would take for me to be carried away by it.

"Seton." His rich baritone voice, which I remembered so well, was saying my name. *How I used to love it when he said my name.* He stood, but seemed to sense that he shouldn't move forward.

"Why are you here?" I choked out. "Why?"

"Seton," he said again. "I've missed you."

Tears sprang to my eyes. *No*, I told myself sternly. *I am not going to cry. He doesn't deserve it.* I had cried over this man more than anything else in my life except my father.

"You don't get to say that," I seethed at him. "You don't get to say that, like you're not the reason for it." *You, who abandoned me in the end, just when I was starting to believe you wouldn't.*

"I'm sorry," he said simply. "Seton, I'm so sorry." He glanced away, and when he looked back to me, I was shocked to notice that his eyes were bright with unshed tears.

"I thought I was doing what was right for you," he said then. "Hell, part of me still thinks that. But..." he took a deep breath and let it out with a small chuckle. "A very bright former prospect told me that I wasn't being fair to you by not letting you make your own decisions about what you wanted."

Anger flooded through me. "No, *I* told you that," I accused. "But you wouldn't listen."

He nodded. "I know. I know. You were right, Seton. I was a hypocrite. But somehow, coming from Cal... it kind of brought it home to me. I'd spent so much time bitching at you about how you weren't letting him grow up. And here I was, treating you like a little girl. But shit, Seton." He shook his head, his shoulders sinking into a defeated slump. "This life... the MC life. It's not good enough for you. You deserve more than some outlaw biker. You have a future." He looked up at me. "Hell, you're gonna be a chef someday!" I opened my mouth to ask how he knew, but he interrupted me. "Cal told me. Plus, I'd know that dent in your fucking car anywhere. I've seen it outside the restaurant. I've driven by it a thousand times by now, hoping to catch a glimpse of you."

He took a few slow steps and stopped about two feet away from me, but kept his arms at his sides as if he could sense I didn't want him to come any closer. "Seton," he said softly. "I'm so sorry. About everything. Especially not telling you about my uncle and your father. It's just… That day. The day your dad was killed. Your eyes have haunted me ever since. You have no idea how many times I've thought about you over the years. And then, when I met you, and realized who you were… it was like I had a second chance to protect that girl. I just couldn't let her risk being hurt by the club again."

Listening to him, my heart began to pound like it was going to leap right out of my chest. Emotions raced through me faster than I could even register what they were: anger, hope, love, fear… "Greyson," I countered, stunned at what I was hearing. "But you told me to let Cal join."

"No. I didn't tell you to let Cal join," he corrected. "I told you to let him make his own choices. And yes, I realize now that I wasn't being consistent. I believe you called me a 'fucking hypocrite,' to be exact." A slight smile came to my lips, and he grinned. "I think I might have also been being a sexist asshole, assuming he could make his own choices but you couldn't."

I resisted the urge to agree with him, and let him continue.

"Seton, sweetheart," he murmured, drawing closer. He raised his hand and softly brushed my cheek with his thumb. "I'll say I'm sorry a million times if you want me to. I was wrong. I know that. But I wasn't wrong about the life you'd be choosing if you were with me." His eyes grew dark, concerned. "There is danger. I'm careful, and the club doesn't take risks unless absolutely necessary, but I'm not a dentist. The club will always be there.

"Once everything Cal and you said had sunk in, I realized I had been so worried about protecting you that I hadn't given you a chance to choose what you wanted," he acknowledged. "But, once I saw what I had done, I couldn't let you choose before you were able to make your decision based on the right things. Not on just how you felt about me. I wanted you to move on with your life, have a shot at something else. Something you wanted, so you could really make your choice. Now, you do.

"So now." He took a step back, his expression solemn. "Now that you have two real choices. Now that I'm not in your life to fuck things up and confuse you. If you still want me..." he spread his hands wide. "If you still want *this*, I'm yours, Seton. I think I always have been."

I stared at him in silence for a moment. What he was saying, it was so big. It felt like the tidal wave again. What Greyson was saying right now, it was exactly what I had wanted to hear all those months ago. It felt surreal to be hearing them now, like I was dreaming the whole thing.

"Greyson," I said quietly. "I don't know if I can forgive you."

A stricken look crossed his face, but then his features rearranged themselves, and suddenly he looked like he could have been discussing how to do an oil change. "I understand," he responded. "I don't want to push you. This is your choice. Your choice alone, this time."

"It's not my choice alone," I said, shaking my head. "It's your choice, too. It's *our* choice. That's the point. That's always been my point."

He looked into my eyes, a soft expression on his face. "Baby, I made my choice a long time ago. I love you, Seton. Always have, always will. But I want you to be happy. I fucked that up once, but I'm not going to do that again. If you're happy without me, so be it. I can love you from far away, too."

"Greyson," I cried, my voice cracking. I threw myself into his arms, the tidal wave breaking over the sea wall. "I choose you," I whispered.

His arms went around me, strong and warm, and he kissed the top of my head, then my forehead, then my tear-wet eyes, then my cheeks, and finally, my lips.

He pulled me to him, kissing me hard at first, and I opened my mouth to his hungrily, as though I had been starving for months and he was feeding me. I reached up and slid my fingers through his hair, and I felt a trickle down my cheek and realized I was crying. Grey must have felt it too, because he pulled away from me for a second and gazed down at me with a serious expression.

"I'll never make you cry again," he whispered, brushing my tears away with his thumbs.

Then he was kissing me again, his mouth persistent, needy. "I missed you so much," he murmured. "Seton."

"I missed you too," I whispered back.

His kisses softened then, making me dizzy with desire. He went slowly, giving me time, and soon I couldn't help myself any more, I tightened my grip on his hair and drew him closer, deeper. His tongue licked against mine, and I answered him eagerly, whimpering softly as heat traveled down my body, growing stronger every second.

He pressed me to him, until I could feel the hardness of his need between us. I bit his bottom lip and smiled to myself as he gasped in response. In a second, somehow we were on the bed, and he was pulling off my black pants and pushing my shirt up over my head. Where a moment ago he was fighting to be patient, now his hands moved quickly to free my breasts from my bra. I lifted myself up on my elbows so he could pull it away, and he let out a loud groan as he looked at me.

"Jesus Christ," he murmured, lowering himself to me. "I've missed this so much."

He took one nipple in his mouth and sucked it gently between his lips, using his tongue to flick and caress. I cried out before I could stop myself, and then giggled, embarrassed at the idea that Carly might have heard me.

From the living room, a voice called, "Okay, then, I'm going out for a while." A second later the door slammed, and both Grey and I collapsed into helpless laughter.

"Shit," he wheezed, "That girl is going to hate me for the rest of her life."

He shook his head, and still smiling, he lowered his mouth to my breasts again. He kissed a path from one to the other, licking the second one in turn. "Gotta give them equal time," he said huskily. I arched my back, pressing my nipple eagerly into his mouth, needing the feel of his expert tongue. My core began to throb, and I could hear myself begin to make low, breathy sounds as I moved under him. I desperately needed him to touch me below, to relieve the ache that had started inside me, which he knew how to soothe so well. I reached down and grabbed the waistband of his jeans, angling my hips against him and spreading my legs wide so that his erection was pressing against my throbbing center. He groaned against my skin as I moved back and forth against him, desperately trying to calm my needful body.

"Greyson," I whispered. "Lose the jeans."

He laughed, loudly. "Okay, then, message received." He rose up and stood, quickly unbuttoning them and letting them fall to the floor, then pulled his shirt over his head in one fluid motion. All my memories of how he looked like this were nothing compared to the reality, and a low sound escaped from my throat as he came back to the bed. I slid my hand around his hardness, stroking him slowly and watching in satisfaction as he threw back his head and moaned. Eagerly, I brought my mouth close to him, and then slowly began to lick around his head as my lips closed over his shaft.

"Christ, Seton," he hissed. His fist went to my hair as I worked him, feeling his cock respond, the skin tightening as he hardened even more under my touch. He looked down at me, unconcealed lust in his eyes. "Good God, I love watching you do that," he said, his voice thick. I continued to suck and swirl. I loved that I could do this to him, how much he wanted me. My mouth began to water at the thought of taking him all the way like that, but he soon pulled away.

"I'm gonna come if you don't stop, and I don't want to like that. Not tonight." He knelt on the bed and lowered himself on top of me. "I've been waiting for you for too long."

He rolled over onto his back then, pulling me with him, and before I knew it I was straddling him, my hands on either side of his head. "I need to taste you," he breathed.

He pushed me forward before I could react, until his face was between my thighs. He grasped my hips in his strong, powerful hands and moved me toward him. I fell forward, my hands bracing against the wall, and he began to lick me. I moaned loudly, so close to exploding already that I couldn't decide whether I wanted him to make me come right then or tease me a little longer.

"Greyson," I whispered urgently, incoherently. "Oh, God…"

He flicked his able tongue just a little faster, then just a little softer, varying the pressure so that he kept me right at the edge, then backed off. I knew my juices were flowing, and he seemed to love it, moaning against my skin as he continued his sweet assault. I squirmed, trying to get closer to his tongue, but he held me fast, refusing to let me come until he was ready. The core of flame inside me began to expand, until it seemed to reach all the way out to the tips of my fingers and the top of my head. He flattened his tongue and licked one final time and I exploded, crying out his name as I came. He continued to lick and lap at me until all of the tension released inside me and I almost fell on top of him, my muscles turning into liquid after being melted by his touch.

Grey sat up then, with me still on top of him, and gently turned me around until my back was pressed to his front. Kneeling on the bed, he lifted me, then set me down so that he entered me as I eased down onto his lap. He groaned loudly as he slid in and my lips closed around him. "If you only knew how many times I've made myself come thinking about this," he murmured into my ear. Slowly, he began to thrust, one arm holding me around my stomach, the other teasing my still-swollen nipples. Having him inside me again is even better than I remembered, and soon the sensation of his cock sliding inside me, hitting my G-spot, made me begin to moan with need all over again. We began to move in a rhythm that was ours alone, as intimate as it was hungry.

"Touch yourself," he commanded, and I did as he said. My fingers found my swollen clit, and I stroked it gently, each stroke making me gasp, and soon I was close to the edge again. I felt his cock grow inside me as he continued to thrust.

"I need you, Greyson," I moaned. "I'm going to come again."

He pushed harder into me, and I arched my back in response, wanting him inside me as far as he could be.

"I'm gonna come inside you," he warned.

"Good. Fill me, Greyson," I urged.

"Fuck, Seton," he growled. "I'm gonna come. Now. Come with me, baby."

I flicked my wet fingers over my clit one more time and hurtled over the edge as I felt him spasm inside me. I came so hard I lost track of everything but the two of us, and it was as though there was no separation between his body and mine, as though we were both just one body shuddering through our release together. I heard him call my name from far away, and then I couldn't think at all for a while, until eventually my orgasm began to fade, and he was holding me in his arms, kissing me.

We lay there lazily afterwards, him twirling a lock of my hair between his fingers. "How long were you waiting here before I showed up?" I asked.

"A couple of hours," he admitted. "I spent the time reading one of your paperbacks, mostly."

"Carly didn't seem like she was much company to you," I smirked.

"Yeah," he chuckled. "I figured it would be best if I left her alone. She almost didn't let me in at all. Damn, she was furious when she opened the door and saw it was me. It took me quite a bit of finagling to get past your doorstep." He kissed the top of my head. "For a while I thought she was gonna call the cops. That girl is fierce."

I grinned. "She is."

We talked some more, then made love again until we were exhausted. Afterwards, we slept, and didn't wake until morning. Carly was still gone when I wandered out into the living room, but had left a note that said simply: "Looks like you guys made up. I'm gone until tomorrow night."

"Shit, I hope she's not mad," I fretted.

"She'll get over it," Grey said. "She was furious with me, but ultimately she just wants you to be happy. She's a good friend."

"She is," I agreed. "Unfortunately, she's not going to be my roommate much longer."

"Why not?" he asked.

"She's got a job in Denver lined up," I explained. "She'll be moving out when our lease is up in two months."

His eyes met mine. "What are you going to do?"

I shrugged. "I guess I'll try to find another roommate. I'll ask around. Or maybe I'll move to another place."

"Oh yeah?" His eyes twinkled. "I got one in mind. Turns out, I'm looking for a roommate, too."

I cocked my head at him. "You don't really seem much like the roommate type."

"Depends on who the roommate is." He reached for me and enfolded me in his arms. "But Seton," he said, his tone growing serious. "I meant what I said earlier. These are your choices. I'm ready for a life with you. God knows I've had enough time to think about it to know there's no one else for me. But I don't want to rush into anything you're not ready for."

"Greyson Stone," I smiled, looking up into his eyes. "I've been ready for you my whole life."

EPILOGUE
GREY

Five Months Later

"See, do you need any help in the kitchen?" I yelled.

"No, don't worry about it!" she called back. "Just see what everyone wants for drinks."

I already knew what most people would be having, so I went out to the garage and grabbed a bunch of beers from the fridge out there. I came back into the living room and handed them around to the brothers and their old ladies. A few of the women opted for wine, including Seton's friends Carly and Andi, and I took care of them, as well. Finally, I went out into the back yard where the kids were and made sure that there were juice boxes all around.

I had just managed to get myself a beer and open one for Seton when she came out into the living room, trays of appetizers in both hands.

"Here you go, everyone!" A loud murmur of approval went up from the men.

"Damn, Grey, we sure have been eating better since you lassoed Seton," Trigger murmured appreciatively as he bit into a ham and cheese croquette. "What are these called again, See?"

"Uhh… fried ham and cheese balls," she said quickly, glancing at me with a small smirk. She knew the brothers would turn up their noses at any food they considered too foofy for an MC member. I winked back at her, the joke staying between just the two of us.

"Why don't you sit down, Seton?" Jules said, waving her hand toward the chair next to me. "Pull up a chair and take a load off. You've been working all day."

"I'll just be a second," Seton nodded. "I have a couple more trays of food to bring out." This was Seton's first time inviting all our "family" over, and she had been having a ball thinking up different foods to serve. A couple of minutes later, she was back with some more goodies with hifalutin' names that would have made the guys' testicles shrink into their sacs if she'd said them. Finally, she flopped down next to me with a sigh. "Oof! There! Finally done for a while."

I smiled and leaned over to kiss her. "It's all great, See. Thanks for doing this."

She smiled, coloring slightly with pleasure. "You know it's my pleasure."

A call went up from the other side of the room. "A toast," Cal announced. "Happy housewarming to Seton and Grey!" The others echoed him, and bottles began to clink as people sealed the toast. I handed Seton the beer I'd gotten her and raised mine to clink against it. She smiled up at me and we drank, eyes locked like we were the only two people in the world.

Andi's voice broke through our private moment. "It's about time you got around to this housewarming party," she complained. "It's been months already since you guys moved in together."

"Hey, we were busy," I complained.

"Yeah," Repo snickered. "Busy getting busy."

"Ain't nothin' wrong with that," Levi said mildly.

"Well, we're happy for you guys," Andi continued. "You were clearly meant for each other."

"Yeah," Carly agreed. "But Grey is lucky he ever got the chance to make this work. The first time I met him, he was storming out of our apartment after Seton kicked him out. The girl cried for *weeks*." She looked straight at me, a memory of her anger visible in her eyes. "I was prepared to kick your ass to next Tuesday if you ever showed up again."

Trigger howled with laughter, and reached over to high-five Carly as the others joined in the merriment. "Oh, man," he cried, slapping his hand against his thigh. "I never thought I'd see the day when a chick would threaten the president of an outlaw biker club and expect to get away with it."

I shot a mock-angry look at Carly. "Hey, I don't hit women," I retorted to Trigger. "Besides which, I'm secure in my masculinity."

"He sure is," Seton murmured, raising her eyebrows suggestively. "And he has a lot of 'masculinity' to be sure of." Laughter erupted again.

The guests were there until well after midnight, and a few stayed to help us clean up, so it was after one o'clock when we finally managed to shut off the lights and get into bed. I made love to Seton long and slow, thinking every second about how fucking lucky I was and that I would never, ever let her go. She was mine. All mine.

Afterward, she lay against me, curled under my arm, her head on my chest. I stroked her hair absently as we talked softly in the darkness.

"God, this is so comfortable," Seton murmured, already half-asleep. She yawned massively. "I'm so, so tired…"

We lay there for a few minutes, neither of us talking. Here we were, settling in to our new house. The first one we'd chosen together. I was happier than I had ever been in my life. It was amazing to think that even eight months ago, I was verbally sparring with a woman who hated the very sight of me. The same woman who was now nestled in my arms, breathing softly and making little noises of contentment.

Seton Greenlee had changed me in so many ways. She made me want to be a better man. A man worthy of her. And I wanted her by my side. Always.

Always.

Almost before I even knew what I was doing, I was kissing the top of her forehead. "Seton, baby," I whispered. "You awake?"

"Mmm…" she murmured. "Just barely."

I hadn't planned this, not at all, but it somehow felt right. Somehow, I didn't want to wait another second to ask her. I hoped she wouldn't be pissed that I wasn't getting down on one knee.

"Seton. Will you marry me?"

She leaned up on her elbow and looked at me, instantly awake. Her eyes were wide, and shone in the moonlight streaming through the window.

"Greyson Stone," she breathed. "Are you proposing to me?"

I grinned at her. "Yeah, I guess I am."

A tear pooled on her lower lashes, and she brushed it away. "My God," she whispered. Her hand reached up to stroke my beard. "Of course I'll marry you, Grey." She chuckled softly. "I didn't think big bad motorcycle men got married."

"They do when they want to make sure their women don't get any bright ideas about skipping town," I growled, burying my face in her neck and nipping at the skin. Seton shrieked.

"Way to ruin the moment, Grey!" she laughed, pushing me away.

"Plus," I continued. "I gotta make sure my babies and their momma all have the same names."

"Babies?" Seton breathed, suddenly serious. Her wide eyes locked on mine.

"Yeah," I nodded. "Babies. And they're all gonna look just like you."

"We'll see about that," she countered, leaning down to kissing me deeply. "I bet they're all going to have their daddy's eyes."

And damned if we didn't start trying to make a baby, right then and there.

Afterwards, we collapsed on the bed, exhausted. "Well, I think that was a pretty good start to creating the Stone family," Seton panted.

"We're gonna have to work hard at this, you know," I warned her. "Making a baby is no picnic. We're gonna try again tomorrow. And the day after that, and the day after that. Probably more than once a day."

She giggled. "Mmmm. Sounds like torture."

"Huh," I tossed back. "I never knew you were into that."

"Shhh," she whispered. "Go to sleep. We need our rest so we can get back to 'work' on project Stone Family in the morning."

I pulled her to me and drew the covers up over the two of us, closing my eyes. "Good night, Mrs. Stone," I whispered.

She sighs contentedly in my arms.

"Good night, Mr. Stone."

RUSH

ACKNOWLEDGMENTS

Every aspiring writer needs people in her corner: to cheer us on, listen to us endlessly talk about characters that we grow to love while we're writing them, and remind us when we're feeling lost that the characters will help us figure out what is supposed to happen to them.

Thank you first of all, to my husband, for being my number one fan and for pushing me to make the jump to full-time writing.

Thank you for my Fourth Friday tribe, who have been my cheerleaders and who have been nothing but supportive of my crazy leap of faith.

And thank you, dear reader, for being the reason I write in the first place.

Books by Daphne Loveling

Motorcycle Club Romance
Los Perdidos MC
Fugitives MC
Throttle: A Stepbrother Romance
Rush: A Stone Kings Motorcycle Club Romance
Crash: A Stone Kings Motorcycle Club Romance
Ride: A Stone Kings Motorcycle Club Romance
Stand: A Stone Kings Motorcycle Club Romance
Ghost: Lords of Carnage MC
Hawk: Lords of Carnage MC
Brick: Lords of Carnage MC
Gunner: Lords of Carnage MC
Thorn: Lords of Carnage MC
Beast: Lords of Carnage MC
Angel: Lords of Carnage MC
Hale: Lords of Carnage MC
Iron Will: Lords of Carnage Ironwood MC
Iron Heart: Lords of Carnage Ironwood MC

Sports Romance
Getting the Down
Snap Count
Zone Blitz

Paranormal Romance
Untamed Moon

ABOUT THE AUTHOR

Daphne Loveling is a small-town girl who moved to the big city as a young adult in search of adventure. She lives in the American Midwest with her fabulous husband and the two cats who own them.

Someday, she hopes to retire to a sandy beach and continue writing with sand between her toes.

Made in the USA
Monee, IL
28 April 2021